THE GILDED CAT

THE GILDED CAT

CATHERINE DEXTER

Morrow Junior Books

NEW YORK

Printed in the United States of America.
1   2   3   4   5   6   7   8   9   10

Library of Congress Cataloging-in-Publication Data
Dexter, Catherine.
The gilded cat / Catherine Dexter.
p.   cm.
Summary: Twelve-year-old Maggie buys a mummified cat at a yard
sale and is drawn into a frightening world of ancient Egyptian magic.
ISBN 0-688-09425-2
[1. Magic—Fiction.   2. Mummies—Fiction.   3. Egypt—Antiquities—
Fiction.]   I. Title.
PZ7.D5387Gi   1992
[Fic]—dc20   91-40784   CIP   AC

For Anna,
Emily,
and
Amanda

THE
GILDED CAT

1

MAGGIE JONES WAS LEANING ON THE kitchen counter reading the newspaper. When she was younger, all she read was the comics. Now that she was twelve, she had branched out to Obituaries and also Metro/Region, which had stories about gory accidents and pets. This particular morning, a sunny Saturday in October, she saw something very interesting in Obituaries.

"Hey, listen to this!"

Maggie's mother was sitting sideways on a kitchen chair giving breakfast to Maggie's two-year-old brother, Spencer. Across the table Maggie's other brother, Tom, who was four, was chewing on a piece of toast. A glob of grape jelly slid off onto his pajama top. He brushed at the jelly, then knocked his toast onto the floor. Minor, the Joneses' dog—a black Lab,

1

mostly—shot out from under the table and gobbled it up.

" 'Mrs. Elmer Wilkins, widow of the renowned archaeologist, died yesterday at Willow Grove Hospital,' " read Maggie. "Isn't her house the one with the greenhouse? I can see it from my window upstairs."

"Where on earth is your father?" said Maggie's mother, reaching for a sponge. "You can have another, Tom, just wait a minute. Maggie, put in another piece of toast for Tom."

Spencer began to howl. He wanted to eat his Cheerios with a fork instead of a spoon.

Maggie shook out the last piece of bread from the plastic bag. It was the heel, but Tom would never notice. She popped it into the toaster and continued reading. " 'A longtime resident of the Parker Hill section of Boston, Mrs. Wilkins accompanied her husband on many of his expeditions to Egypt.' "

"All right, you can try it just this once," Maggie's mother said to Spencer.

Maggie sighed and folded up the paper. She might as well be reading to a stone. There was nothing really good in the paper anyway. What she liked best were articles about unexplained events—poltergeists in Maine, evidence of ESP, people who turned up by the roadside with amnesia (could they be aliens in

2

disguise?). She cut out the best ones and kept them in a folder in her desk. She had once gotten ahold of a wonderful newspaper called the *Star,* which was full of precisely the news she liked best, but her parents had found it and made her throw it out.

The toaster popped. Maggie pulled out the toast, slapped a little margarine on it, and set it on the table in front of Tom. Then she tried to melt inconspicuously from her mother's sight, slipping around to the back stairs just off the kitchen and climbing them two at a time toward her room.

"Maggie?" The voice followed her. "I'm going to need you to help this morning! Don't stay up there too long!"

Maggie gently closed her door and took a deep breath in the silence. Her room was off-limits to her brothers, and her parents hardly ever came up, either. It had once been a maid's room and was by itself on the third floor. The second floor of their house was a separate apartment that they rented to a pair of doctors. This fall the doctors were away on a study grant, and Maggie loved the feeling that she was all by herself in the top part of the house. Kitchen noises came straight up the stairwell, but she could always shut her door.

Maggie had arranged her furniture herself, squeezing her bed into one alcove, with her desk around the corner from it. On the back of her closet door was a full-length mirror with a wavy place in the middle. She caught a glimpse of herself in it—curly dark hair that never looked combed and didn't now either, and clothes like everybody wore: sweatpants, a huge T-shirt, and running shoes. She was already two inches taller than her mother, and her feet were bigger, too.

She stepped over to the window and looked across through the treetops to the roof of Mrs. Wilkins's house. Archaeologists collected interesting, weird things. Now that the old woman was no longer there, the house seemed unprotected. Maggie couldn't help wondering what had been left inside.

She shook her head. She already had plans for today, if she could just get out of baby-sitting and chores for a while. She got her wallet out of her top bureau drawer and counted the bills. Then she pulled on a sweater and went quietly back downstairs.

"Hi! Bye!" she called into the kitchen, hoping not to be stopped.

"Where are you going?" asked her mother over Spencer's screams. He sat in front of his bowl of cereal, clutching a fork in his fist and kicking his chair as he tried to harpoon individual Cheerios.

4

Tom had disappeared, leaving a purple smear across the table.

"Over to Chestnut Street. There's a yard sale. That O'Connell family—they're moving."

"The O'Connells? I hadn't heard that."

"Kelly Ryan told me."

"Where did you see her? I wonder if she still baby-sits."

"She works up at the drugstore now, Mom. It pays twice as much."

"Well, nobody will be sorry to see the O'Connells go."

"And what lucky neighborhood is going to get them?" said Maggie's father, who had just gotten up. He came padding across the kitchen in his bedroom slippers and bathrobe.

"Kelly said they're going to Florida. Can I go now?"

"I guess," said her mother. "But I need you to baby-sit later on. Why don't you take Minor? He needs a walk."

"He'd just knock stuff over."

"Don't be gone too long."

"Right," said Maggie, and slipped out the back door before her mother could think of something else.

Parker Street was wide and busy and lined on both sides with big two-family houses. Most of the houses had old people living in them or groups of graduate students or couples with babies. There was nobody Maggie's age nearby; her best friend from school, Julie MacDougall, lived on the other side of the city.

The O'Connells lived two blocks away. They had two teenage boys who used to break into houses in the neighborhood. Everybody knew it, but nobody had been able to catch them. They stole jewelry and cameras and watches, things they could back out of a window with. Then the older boy got sent to Florida to live with his grandmother—probably even his parents couldn't stand him—and the robberies had stopped.

The O'Connells had spread their possessions on tables and blankets on the ground all along their driveway. No one was there yet. Maggie hoped she wouldn't be noticed right away and put on the spot about buying something. She walked past a card table crowded with dishes and a greasy waffle iron and some *Reader's Digest* condensed books with the jackets still perfect. Leaning against the table were a pair of pink plastic flamingos, the kind people stick in the grass in front of their house. Seemed like they ought to be taking those with them to Florida.

Right next to the flamingos was a box marked

ANYTHING HERE FIFTY CENTS. Maggie stooped over to pick through the box. Here were the really pitiful, ragged ends of the household—a dented pot, a softball full of tooth marks, and something wrapped in a piece of cloth, something that looked up at Maggie with round black eyes.

Maggie stared back at the eyes for a moment and then gingerly pulled the thing out. It was a little figure of some sort, wrapped in a doll blanket. She shook the blanket loose and saw what looked vaguely like a cat all bundled up, with pointed ears and eyes painted on. It might have been made of papier-mâché.

Maggie glanced toward the house. An older lady wearing a housedress and a man's gray sweater came out of the front door and began arranging something on a table set up at the foot of the driveway. A moment later a sleepy-looking boy, tall, with straight blond hair sticking up, came out and flung himself into the folding chair behind the table.

The woman talked to the boy, then turned, saw Maggie, and hurried toward her. "Is that there something you want? I hope you've got the exact price, because we don't have any change yet." She looked at what Maggie was holding. "Oh," she said. "Is that all?"

"What is it?" asked Maggie.

The woman shrugged her shoulders. "I think it was one of the kids made that in school, you know, when he was younger. Kindergarten. Not much to look at, is it? Still, you never know." She gave a laugh and moved off toward the open garage. Maggie could see a bald man, probably Mr. O'Connell, shoving a ratty armchair around inside the garage.

By now another person had come to the yard sale, a man wearing a brown cloak, and Maggie was sure he was looking at her. She was suddenly afraid that someone else would get the little statue, and she definitely wanted it.

Maggie walked down to the end of the driveway, where the boy presided over a shoe box. He looked about fourteen or fifteen. She glanced at his face—he had mean green eyes—and she knew that he had never in his born days made this thing. She dug into her wallet for two quarters and handed him the money.

"You can't bring this back if you change your mind," he said. "You buy it, it's yours."

"I do want it," Maggie said.

"You got it." The boy tilted back on two legs of his chair and whistled to show how bored he was.

"Right," said Maggie, and she quickly turned away. As she started up the sidewalk, though, she glanced down at the creature, and its eyes began to bother her. She was holding it in the crook of her arm, and she felt it looking up at her.

She went back to the boy with the shoe box.

"You hear what I said? You can't bring it back." He came sharply down on all four legs of his chair.

"I wasn't! All I want's a bag to put it in." His insistence was making her nervous. He almost made her think she *should* give it back.

"Ma!" the boy bawled over his shoulder.

Mrs. O'Connell looked up from a box of clothes.

"We got a bag?"

Maggie felt her face turn red. She hated asking a stranger for something. Her dad was exactly the same way. If they got lost driving, he would stay lost all day rather than ask somebody for directions.

"Here you go," said Mr. O'Connell, meekly emerging from the garage. He had an armful of brown grocery bags.

"Thanks," said Maggie, taking one and shaking it open. She shoved the figure inside and rolled the top down. Then she walked away as fast as she could. The O'Connells gave her the creeps, and it was all she could do to keep from running. She could tell the boy was watching her as she walked self-consciously all the way up the street.

2

BY THE TIME MAGGIE REACHED HER
own house, she felt completely spooked. Her breath
was suddenly gone, and there was no reason for it.
She made herself climb slowly up to her room and
close the door and sit down on the edge of the bed.
She looked at the brown grocery bag. What was
going on? This was just a regular Saturday morning,
and that was just a plain old yard sale.

When she had calmed down, she unrolled the top
of the bag and took out the figure. Up close, she
wasn't so sure what animal it was supposed to be. Its
triangular ears stood up the way a cat's did, but its
body was all wound into a smooth bundle. Its round
black eyes still seemed to look at her. She held it for
a moment in the palms of her hands, the way she
would a new kitten, and then had the distinct feeling
that she had insulted it.

10

She stood up, annoyed and a little shaken. She left it on her pillow and went downstairs.

"Hi, Pop." Her father was reading the newspaper, oblivious to the tipped-over cereal box, the scattered spoons and jam-jar tops, the cabinet doors hanging open. A mug of coffee steamed pleasantly by his elbow, and a spiral of smoke wafted up from his pipe.

"Your mother has gone for groceries, but she left us our orders. I'm supposed to empty the dishwasher. You're supposed to put away your clean laundry." Maggie could see stacks of her turtlenecks and underwear and rolled-up socks on the dining room table. From her brothers' room came the sound of a slap and a wail that peaked like a siren. Spencer stubbed up the hall on bare feet, his diaper waggling behind, his face red with indignation. "Tom took it!"

Mr. Jones gathered Spencer up onto his bathrobed knee and jiggled him, lifting the newspaper a little higher so he could see it over Spencer's head. One of Maggie's father's best characteristics was that he was patient. He was almost too patient. He never got mad—Maggie's mother did that; and he never worried or fussed about things the way she did. He just went calmly on.

Her father reached around Spencer to turn the newspaper page. "Any treasures?" he asked her.

11

"I got one thing, but I don't know if it's exactly a treasure. Want to see?"

"Sure."

Maggie climbed back up the stairs to her room. As she stepped across the threshold, she thought she heard something, a rustling noise, like an animal moving. She stopped dead. Last summer they had had a bat. Maggie had woken in the middle of the night to see a dark shape circling and circling in her room, just like in the movies. It didn't make a sound, yet its silhouette kept appearing against the streetlit window, and then its shadow would fall across a blank wall. Maggie had dived under her covers and stayed there until morning.

At first her parents had told her she was dreaming. Then they said that if there had been a bat, it was long gone now. As they had stood in the kitchen arguing about it, a small brown form had come hurtling at them up the length of the front hall. Maggie's mother had screamed the loudest. "I told you!" Maggie had exclaimed. It had taken her father half an hour of swiping with a broom to drive it out a window. It had lain on the ground, apparently dead. Maggie had watched it for a while, and then finished her breakfast. When she looked again, it was gone.

Maggie crossed the room quickly, grabbed the

yard-sale cat, left the room, and closed the door behind her. She ran down the stairs faster than she meant to. Spencer wriggled off their father's knee and disappeared down the hall as Maggie handed over the cat. "What do you think?"

Her father turned it in his hands and chuckled. "Well, this is quite something. You know what it reminds me of? See how it's wrapped in strips of cloth? That's how mummies look."

"Mummies?"

"You know—from Egypt. Those Egyptians, they mummified everything, not just people. They made mummies of dogs and birds and crocodiles. Even baboons." Maggie's father knew all sorts of odd things. He spent a lot of time reading, and it seemed as if he never forgot anything he read.

"You mean this has a dead animal inside it?"

"Could be!" Her father laughed. "Well, it's pretty unlikely that you'd come across a real mummy that's thousands of years old. Still—I remember once, years ago, someone stole a gold earring from the Museum of Fine Arts—a Greek earring, I think it was—and the whole city was in an uproar until it was found, hidden in a tin can in a park nearby. It was even written up in *Newsweek* and *Time*. What we ought to do is go to the museum and do a bit of research. They've got a huge Egyptian collection. Haven't you ever been to the mummy room? I thought all schoolkids went there."

"We were supposed to go in fifth grade, but we had a new teacher and she took us to Pilgrim Village instead."

"We'll have to go then, maybe tomorrow. And then we could consult our neighbor Mrs. Wilkins. Her husband was an archaeologist, and I believe ancient Egypt was his specialty. She's probably seen a million of these."

"I saw in the paper this morning that she died," said Maggie.

"Oh, no! I missed that." Maggie's father began turning through the second section of the newspaper. He folded back the obituary page.

"There's Mom," said Maggie.

Her father put down the paper and walked outside, still in his bathrobe, to help with the groceries. Maggie half hoped no one saw him, though he did look imposing. He sometimes did things—like walking outdoors in his bathrobe—that were embarrassing, but also made her want to laugh.

Maggie's mother wasn't laughing. "Those porch steps will break completely through one of these days," she said as she carried in the first bag. "This house is falling apart."

"Did you see that Mrs. Wilkins died?" asked Maggie's father, following her in with three bulging bags.

"Yes, Maggie told me this morning, while you were still in bed." Mrs. Jones began to unpack the groceries on the kitchen counter. "I wonder what they'll do with the house. Try to make condominiums, I bet. They'll never sell it to a family."

"Why not?" asked Maggie. "I'd like to live there."

"These go in the bathroom closet." Maggie's mother handed Maggie a stack of toilet-paper rolls. She lined up boxes of crackers, cans of chicken soup, a big orange jug of detergent. Maggie went down the hall and put the toilet paper away. "Because it will be too expensive. Who would pay half a million dollars to live on Webster Road?"

"Who would pay that to live anywhere?" muttered Mr. Jones.

"Good gracious—what is that?" Maggie's mother had just noticed the bundle on the kitchen table.

"It's what I got at the yard sale," answered Maggie. "It might be a mummy, Dad says."

"It could be thousands of years old," added her father in a lofty voice.

"Fine," said Maggie's mother. "But get it off my kitchen table."

Maggie carried it up to her room and closed the door. She could still hear her parents' voices in the

15

distance, tense and argumentative, but she didn't have to hear the words. As she stood in the silence, an uneasy sensation prickled across her shoulders. The room had a funny stirred-up feeling, as if someone had just left it.

Maggie put the figure on her desk top. It gave her a shiver to think that this hard, whitish bundle might once have been a live cat or dog, walking around in Egypt, and now its bones were lying right on her blotter.

She kind of hoped her dad was wrong.

Maggie decided to call Julie MacDougall later that afternoon, while she was baby-sitting for Tom and Spencer. The boys were in the side yard, so Maggie brought the phone over to the window to keep an eye on them. Tom was trying to get Spencer to play Batman and Robin, but Spencer wouldn't keep on his mask. Maggie dialed Julie's number.

"What are you doing?" Maggie asked.

Julie popped her gum. "I've got to go shopping in a while. I'm going to get a sweatshirt and some sweatpants, and also underwear—my mom says my underwear's a disgrace, but she's pretty picky. How about you?"

"I went to a yard sale."

"Was it any good?" Julie loved yard sales, too.

"Mostly old pots and stuff, no jewelry, but I got this one thing, a weird little statue. My dad says it could be a mummy."

"Are you serious?"

"It's shaped like a mummy, and it looks old."

"So are you going to open it?"

"Yuck—no! Dad's going to take me to the museum to see if it looks like the real thing. Maybe we'll go tomorrow. Want to come along?"

"Sure. We could go to the museum shop—they've got lots of great stuff, like posters and earrings."

"Listen, I have to go. The kids are fighting. Call me when you get back."

"Bye," said Julie.

Maggie hung up and went outside. Spencer was flailing around with a plastic baseball bat, and Tom was standing out of striking range and yelling at him. Maggie managed to grab one end of the bat. "We don't hit people," she said. "I'll take this away if you hit Tom with it."

"Can't we go to the playground? I want to go to the playground," whined Tom. "It's no fun with Spencer, he's such a baby."

"I guess we could go." Maggie sighed. The playground was the world's most boring spot, but at least there would be other kids there, and all she'd have to do is give the boys a cracker once in a while.

"I don't want to!" said Spencer.

"You'll like it when we get there," said Maggie.

"No! I won't!"

Maggie scooped him up, kicking feet and all, and carried him inside. He would change his mind. He always loved the playground.

She locked the windows, wrote a note to her parents, and stuffed some crackers into a plastic bag. "Go use the bathroom," she reminded Tom. Spencer followed him, and in a moment they emerged, Tom needing his pants snapped but otherwise ready to go.

"Wait here one sec, I'm going to get a book," Maggie said. She ran up the stairs—and remembered, just in time, the rustling noises from the morning. She opened her door slowly and checked the corners of the ceiling: nothing. Tom was starting to thump up the stairs. "Wait down there," she called, and began hastily scanning her bookshelves for something good. Tom appeared in the doorway.

"Why didn't you wait downstairs?" snapped Maggie. She didn't want him noticing the mummy on her desk and asking what was it and could he play with it. "Now let's go."

"Look!" said Tom. "A bird!" He pointed behind Maggie.

She turned. It was sitting on her desk lamp,

perched lightly on the metal shade. Its body was plump, its feathers sleek and black; but the worst part was that it had a human head, a bird-size human head, and it was smiling. Maggie heard a scraping sound as its talons slipped and then tightened their grasp on the edge of the lamp shade.

Maggie grabbed Tom around the waist and charged downstairs. She shoved him onto the porch, pushed Spencer out beside him, and slammed the back door. Her heart beat wildly, and she was shaking from head to toe. Too late, she saw that the back-door key was still inside. Too bad. That was where it was going to stay. The house could just go unlocked.

"What was that in your room?" asked Tom.

"Nothing. I don't know."

"Did you let it in?"

"No! I don't know what you saw. And don't tell." She only wanted to get as far away from the house as she could.

They stayed at the playground for an hour. In a bit a man came and sat down on the next bench over. He didn't do anything like read a newspaper or smoke a pipe; he just sat there, glancing at her every now and then. It made Maggie even more nervous than she already was, though she knew she was safe, because there were other grown-ups at the playground with their toddlers. He looked like the man at the yard sale, wearing that odd brown cloak. Nobody wore a cloak nowadays, nobody that Maggie had ever seen. After a while he got up and walked away, but even after he was gone, Maggie felt that he was still there, as if he had left his imprint in the air.

When they finally walked home, Maggie was relieved to see her parents' car already in the driveway.

"Maggie, did you know you left the door unlocked?" asked her mother.

"Woops!" She hoped she sounded surprised.

"That's the first time you've ever done that."

"The boys were fighting, and I guess I was in a hurry."

"Next time be more careful."

"Can Julie sleep over tonight?"

"It's fine with me. We're going out, so you'd probably like the company."

"You're going out? Where? How late?"

"Just the movies. There's a Bogart film showing that we used to see in college. Now how about putting that laundry away?"

Maggie groaned. She picked up the stacks of clean clothes from the dining room table and started to climb the back stairs. Halfway up, she stopped. She put the clothes on one side of the stairs and went back down.

Julie called at supper time. She said that she couldn't sleep over, because her mother thought she was coming down with a cold. She could come tomorrow morning, though, if she was feeling all right.

"So this means I've got to stay here all by myself?" Maggie fumed.

"We won't be late," said her mother.

Maggie picked the mushrooms off her pizza. "I'm staying up till you get home," she said.

At nine o'clock Maggie stood at the foot of the stairs going up to her bedroom. The boys had fallen asleep in front of the television set, and she had spread quilts over them where they lay. She wanted to watch the nine o'clock movie, but every time she sat down to get comfortable, she thought of the pile of laundry and of what might be at the top of the stairs.

She had started up twice and turned around before she got to the stack of clothes. If she put it off any longer, she would miss part of the movie. She wanted to know that there was nothing up there. She *had* to know.

The best thing to do was go as fast as possible, like yanking off a Band-Aid. She took a deep breath and ran up, two steps at a time, grabbed the clean shirts and underwear, and kept on going. She wrenched open the door and burst across the threshold. The room was completely dark except for a purplish patch of light from the street lamp. She groped for the light switch, humming loudly to cover up any noises that she might not want to hear.

The mummy was right where she had left it on her desk, its eyes just black, painted circles, completely lifeless. Otherwise, her room was empty. The bird thing, whatever it was, was gone—she didn't see it, and she knew it was gone.

She left the clean clothes in the middle of her bed, then carefully closed the door to her room and went back down to watch the movie.

3

___

A COLD WIND BLEW UP OVERNIGHT, and by morning it was raining—a drenching, freezing, blowing, miserable rain. Maggie hadn't slept very well, and she felt scratchy and awful when she got up. She took a quick glance at the so-called mummy and decided it looked like nothing but an inconsequential lump of plaster. Her father made breakfast, and she began to cheer up as she tasted the warm maple syrup filling each sunken waffle square.

Julie's mother dropped her off at nine-thirty. Julie was carrying two notebooks in a blue canvas bag, and under her new yellow slicker she was wearing a new sweat suit—pearly gray with white stitching.

Julie shed her raincoat and did a handstand in the front hall. She had been taking gymnastics since she was four years old, and by now she was really good.

23

She was small and limber, the way gymnasts were supposed to be.

"Well, you're looking mighty sprightly!" said Maggie's dad as he came out to greet Julie. He had some countryish sayings that he liked to use around Maggie's friends. "Want some waffles?"

"No, thanks. I already had breakfast."

"Are you up for a trip to the museum?"

Julie grinned and shrugged her shoulders. "Fine." She was Mr. Jones's favorite of Maggie's friends, and she liked him, too.

"Let's go up to my room," said Maggie. Julie hung her dripping slicker behind the kitchen door and followed Maggie upstairs. She noticed the mummy right away.

"Is this what you got?" She picked it up, turned it over in her hands, shook it. "Looks like a baby piñata. It kind of stares at you, doesn't it?" Maggie peered over Julie's shoulder, but to her it seemed that the "look" was gone.

It took an hour for Maggie's father to finish reading the Sunday *Globe,* have another cup of coffee, and find the museum membership card. At last they were on their way, windshield wipers flapping, rain drumming loudly on the car roof.

"We're off to see the mummy, the wonderful

mummy of Oz," sang Mr. Jones. Julie laughed, but Maggie didn't.

The Museum of Fine Arts faced the street. Out in front was a famous statue of a Native American sitting on a horse and stretching his arms toward the sky. Maggie could barely see him through the car's fogged-up windows. They parked in the museum's lot and dashed through the rain to the entrance. After they'd checked their raincoats at the cloakroom, Maggie's father unfolded a guide map. Maggie gazed around at the entranceway, with its marble floor and vaulted ceiling; an enormous painting, of nothing but colors, hung on one giant wall.

"The mummy room is on the first floor," said Mr. Jones, stuffing the map into his pocket. They tramped after him through galleries and down corridors, past display cases of South American necklaces and rooms of gleaming old furniture. Maggie was getting butterflies in her stomach. She wasn't sure she wanted to come upon someone dead, even all wrapped up. Finally they came to a doorway with a small sign, a joke: a drawing of a bandaged hand with one pointing finger and the words TO THE MUMMIES.

The wooden floor creaked beneath Maggie's feet as she stepped into the room. The walls were painted dark green, and soft spotlights shone on display

25

cases, on a few small Egyptian statues, on a huge stone sarcophagus, and on a large glass case in the middle of the room. A group of children and parents was clustered around the case. Maggie peered past their shoulders. In the case lay two mummies, side by side, wrapped in bandages stained with age. One was so small it must have been a child. The other was small, too—maybe the Egyptians had been short. A card beside the mummy's feet identified it as a woman. It was hard to believe a real person lay in the center of that bundle, her feet pointing straight up. Could she have guessed three thousand years ago that one day she'd be lying here?

Maggie turned away, toward the small cases ranged along the walls. Soft lights shone on tiny objects, bits of gold, only half an inch across, hammered into animal shapes—a hippopotamus, a falcon, a crocodile. There were four jars painted a glossy turquoise blue, with animal heads for tops. There was a brownish wrapped lump that was labeled the mummy of a ram. And then she saw it, tucked in the back corner. *Mummy of a Kitten*, the tag read. *Animals were sometimes sacrificed and their mummies included in royal tombs.* It looked exactly the same as the thing Maggie had bought.

Maggie tugged Julie over by the sleeve. Julie gasped so loud that other people in the room turned to look at her. "You do have a mummy!" she squealed. The two girls huddled together, trying to stifle their giggles.

Maggie's father had stopped by the entrance and was studying a huge painting of some nineteenth-century scientists dissecting a mummy. He turned when he heard the commotion, and Maggie beckoned him over. "There it is!" she said.

"Well, what do you know." Mr. Jones stared into the display case, then began to pat his pockets, searching for his pipe. "Who would've believed it?" He found his pipe, looked at it, put it back in his jacket pocket.

"Maybe there's a reward!" said Julie.

"We'll have to bring it in and find out," said Maggie's father. "Of course, it could be a fake. But why would anyone counterfeit something like that? Tell you what. I'm going outside for a minute to smoke my pipe. You two can stay here and look some more. Just don't wander off and get lost. I'll be back in ten minutes."

The crowd of children and parents had vanished by now, and even the guard who had been at the door had gone. The room was dark, with its glossy black-green walls. Pools of warm light fell peacefully on the ancient objects. Other cases gleamed with gold jewelry and tiny animals carved from colored stone. Maggie couldn't stop staring at the mummified kitten. She didn't like to think of them wrapping it in strips of white linen, with its little paws folded over and its eyes shut tight. She hoped hers had been dead to begin with and wasn't one of the sacrificial ones.

There was a constant hum in the room from the humidity control, so Maggie didn't hear the footsteps behind her. Yet she suddenly knew that someone was standing there, someone dark and gaunt, with burning eyes.

Maggie made herself turn around. It was only a friendly-looking fellow, about her height, slightly plump, with a fringe of light brown hair. Something about him seemed familiar. He was going bald, and he had a pointed nose that was pink on the end. His glasses kept sliding down, and his pants seemed about to fall off. He suddenly cleared his throat. Maggie jumped a mile.

"Sorry! I didn't mean to startle you," he said. "You've been standing here for such a long time, I couldn't help noticing. Most people just take a look at the mummies and go."

He was standing awfully close to her. Maggie backed up a step. She couldn't quite see his eyes, because his glasses reflected the light. Julie had gone to the other side of the room and was looking at a

stone figure of Osiris, god of the Egyptian Underworld.

"Everybody loves Egyptian things, don't they?"
he said, clearing his throat again. Maggie nodded and
swallowed with a little crackling sound. He leaned
close to her, and Maggie noticed that he wore a tiny
gold earring in one ear. It was shaped like a snake.
"I couldn't help hearing what you were saying. It's
not so unusual as you may think for someone to
come across an Egyptian relic. At one time they
were cheap. Even mummies were sold for next to
nothing."

"I got mine at a yard sale," said Maggie. Out of the
corner of her eye she saw Julie look over at the sound
of her voice. Maggie turned her back, as if to shut
Julie out.

"That was lucky," the man said. "Now you must
find out everything you can about it. The museum
is a wonderful place to study the Egyptians. We have
an enormous collection. I am the curator, by the
way. My name is Seth Morgan. And you are—?"

"Maggie Jones."

"Pleased to meet you." He extended his hand for
Maggie to shake. It felt oddly dry and bony, though
it looked plump.

"I could show you some very interesting things in
the basement, if you like," he said. "We're working

on an exhibit that will show a complete burial chamber for a royal prince. Most of it is reconstructed, of course. We've never had a genuine burial chamber, complete, among our holdings. We came close, though. On his last expedition, Professor Elmer Wilkins discovered the tomb of Thutmose the Utmost, a boy pharaoh who ruled such a short time that his reign was never recorded in history. We don't know how he died. Unfortunately for the museum, Thutmose's entire tomb was lost during shipment back to this country."

"Lost?" said Maggie. "How could you lose a whole tomb?" Julie was inching closer, but Maggie acted as if she didn't see her.

"We know it reached these shores. Professor Wilkins brought a boatload of cartons back with him. He had workrooms here, in the basement, where his helpers sorted through his finds and labeled them. But this particular shipment never arrived. People speculated that the crates were lifted onto the wrong loading dock at the harbor and shipped to some other port. We may never know."

"We live close to where Professor Wilkins lived," said Maggie. "Mrs. Wilkins just died."

"No wonder you're interested in ancient Egypt! Did you know that over the centuries thousands and thousands of objects have been found and lost again?

People have been robbing the tombs of kings ever since the first one was buried. The earth is full of Egyptian relics, carried here, carried there, sold many times over. Some of the most beautiful and the most powerful have been lost forever."

"How could a relic be powerful?" asked Maggie. Julie stopped a few feet away, waiting to be acknowledged.

"If it had the natural power of magic," said Morgan. "The Egyptians still had the ancient knowledge of magic—for them it wasn't so old. All Egyptians, even ordinary laborers, even children, knew about magic. What else are all these for?" He waved his hand at the cases of tiny animals and carvings. "Amulets, for protection. There were magicians in Egypt, too, and they had far greater powers than these bits of stone. They could transform their appearance, call up powers of the earth and of the animal kingdom. They weren't just entertainers, like the weak magicians you see today."

"That's nice," said Maggie lamely. She was beginning to think protectively of that little wrapped blob on her desk at home. If it was a real relic, how many times had it been lost and found throughout history? What might its powers be? She didn't necessarily want to give it back. Maybe it liked being found by her.

"Take that little cat you say you have. It was probably part of a royal burial chamber. Who knows? Perhaps it's part of the missing tomb!"

Maggie's heart thudded hard.

"You really ought to find out where it came from."

Maggie didn't think the O'Connells had been to Egypt, and Mrs. O'Connell sure didn't have an idea what the cat was. Their son was dying to get rid of it. Come to think of it, though, it was odd the way he almost yelled at her about not bringing it back.

"I'm busy later this afternoon, so if you would like to see that exhibit, you must come now."

Seth Morgan strode away.

"Wait! I do want to come!" Maggie said. As she raced across the room after Morgan, she wondered why she was doing this. But why not? Nothing bad could happen in a museum, of all places. She didn't look back, though she knew Julie was standing there. She pushed through a door marked STAFF ONLY and found herself on a staircase landing. Morgan was already out of sight, but his footsteps echoed in the stairwell. "Down here!" his voice floated up to her. Maggie hesitated. She had the momentary impression that the gaunt figure was standing near her again. But there was no one there, only the empty metal stairs leading up and down.

4

SETH MORGAN WAS WAITING FOR MAG-
gie two landings below. As soon as he saw her, he
pushed through a door and walked quickly along
some carpeted corridors. Maggie hurried to keep up.
The halls were painted a smooth ivory, and most of
the doors they passed were closed. It was strangely
quiet, as if everything were padded.

Sometimes Maggie would come to an open door,
hear a burst of voices, see heads turn in her direction;
then she'd be past and hurrying around more corners, through another door with frosted glass, down
more stairs.

Now the lights had become bare bulbs stuck in the
ceiling. The walls were cinder blocks, and the floor
was dingy tile. She walked as fast as she could, but
she could barely keep Morgan in sight.

Finally he stopped to unlock a tall wire door, like

the opening to an enormous cage. He flipped on a light switch, and they stepped into a tangle of shelves and tables and dim doorways. Metal shelves like the ones Maggie's father had in their garage lined the walls, and on them rested stacks of coffin-sized boxes. Against another wall were rows of shallow drawers with cryptic labels, and beside them were shelves crowded with tiny things—miniature statues and bits of bright stone—each sitting on a typed label. On a table in the corner some long pieces of yellowed paper were laid out. A smell of dreadful age was in the air.

"What's in those?" Maggie pointed to a row of square boxes shaped like hatboxes and covered with dust.

"Mummy heads," said Morgan. "You don't want to see them."

Maggie walked over to an open door and peered around it. There lay a mummy, flat out on a long table, with a paper cup half full of coffee by its feet. "It's just lying there!" she gasped.

"Yes, well, our work space is not ideal," said Morgan. He pointed to the long pieces of paper. "I have to work on the scrolls in such poor light." He leaned over and spoke close to her ear. "Do you know what these are? Have you ever heard of the Book of the Dead?"

The Book of the Dead? Maggie glanced over at the mummy, which suddenly looked like a knowing presence. The basement was so quiet, and nobody knew she was here. What if Morgan was going to do something awful? What if he killed her? He could just pop her into one of those coffinish boxes and she wouldn't be found for centuries. He smelled so peculiar, like an empty church. And another thing—he was wearing sandals. She had just noticed. Sandals with a suit. She could see his bare toes sticking right out underneath his trouser cuffs.

Maggie shook her head.

"The Egyptians themselves called it the Book of Coming Forth by Day. They believed that the human soul lived on after death, just as many religions do today. They thought the Afterlife was like real life on earth, only better. But to get there, each person's soul had to journey through the Underworld and pass through many gates guarded by monsters and horrible gods. The Book of Coming Forth by Day contains all the spells the soul needs to complete its journey safely. Scrolls like these were often put into royal tombs. Would you like me to teach you to read them?"

"That's okay. I'm not too good even at Spanish," stammered Maggie. She looked at the rows and rows of little drawings and scratchings on the scrolls. She recognized owls and stick figures and snakes and chicks and eyes. She saw something else, too. In the margin was an illustration of a mummy lying on a couch, and over it hovered a bird with a man's head. "What's this?" she asked.

"That's the *ba*-bird," said Morgan. "One form of the spirit. After death it can fly around in the world of the living. Why does that interest you?"

Maggie shook her head. She wasn't ready to tell anyone yet.

"There's another form of the soul, too, called the *ka*. It stays in the tomb with the person's mummy and looks exactly like that person did during life. The soul can assume a third form, the *akh*, when it enters the blessed Fields of Reeds or, some say, has become a star in the sky. But before it can do that, it has to go through all the gates of the Underworld and appear in the Hall of Judgment before forty-two gods and answer questions about its life on earth. Its heart is put in a set of scales and weighed against the Feather of Truth." He pointed to another drawing. "If the speaker tells a lie, the balance tips against his heart, and his heart is devoured on the spot by Ammit, that creature there, who is part lion, part crocodile, part hippopotamus. Then that person will never reach the Afterlife; he is destroyed forever. It was the worst possible fate."

36

"Even if you only told a small lie?"

"The scrolls tell exactly how to answer so that you don't make any mistakes. Then your soul goes on to the Fields of Reeds, where there are never any hardships. If the person has been buried properly, with plenty of shawabtis, he doesn't even have to do a lick of work." Morgan opened one of the shallow drawers and showed Maggie row after row of little clay figures. They looked like chessmen. "These are shawabtis, the servants who do all the work in the Afterlife. All our kings and rich people are buried with these."

"Are you Egyptian, too?"

Morgan cleared his throat three times. "I sometimes think I am. That's always happening to us Egyptologists. We start to think we're personal friends with our mummies and pharaohs, our pots and shards." He gave a happy little hum. "Now what I wonder is—" He stopped and put his hands on his hips and looked at Maggie quizzically. "What I wonder is—how interested you really are in Egyptian religion and magic. The two went together thousands of years ago. Something tells me you are very interested, and that you even have some aptitude for it. I don't suppose—?"

"You don't suppose what?"

"Well." He seemed to be making up his mind. He

37

lowered his voice. "I suspect that the mummy you found *is* an important artifact. Quite possibly it once belonged to this young Thutmose. Perhaps his soul still roams the earth, looking for it!"

"That's not him in there, is it?" Maggie asked. She was beginning to feel very confused.

"No, no, no. That's Muthetepti, a singer of no importance. She's waiting for X rays. As I told you, the whereabouts of Thutmose's mummy are a mystery. Perhaps your task is to return the kitten mummy to its owner." Seth Morgan sounded as if he had already made up his mind about it. "Everything in a burial chamber is there for a purpose, either to help the person get to the Afterlife or for him to enjoy once he arrives. Royal children were even buried with their favorite toys. You will make the soul of Thutmose very happy if you return his pet to him. From studying these scrolls I have come to believe that Thutmose's tomb is actually quite near. Perhaps you will be guided to it."

"Would this be dangerous?" Maggie asked nervously. "What would I have to do?"

"There are certain rituals you will have to perform, and that's where the magic will come in handy. You may even change your mind or wish to run away, and the spells will help you know what to do and have the strength to do it."

It seemed as though Morgan had already decided for her. Maggie began to picture a room heaped with jewels and golden furniture—an unbelievable treasure, and she would be the one to discover it.

"I'll teach you some of the protective spells. The ancient formulas are quite simple."

When she hesitated, Morgan added impatiently, "Most children would think this was a wonderful opportunity."

"My father's probably wondering where I am."

"You've only been gone a few minutes." He rested his hands on the table in front of her, and she noticed for the first time that he wore a ring on his little finger. It was shaped like a snake. She blinked, and the snake slithered once around his finger: a snake as green as a blade of grass. Then it was a ring again. In the stillness Maggie heard a faint scratching sound, like something dry scraping along the floor.

"Okay," she whispered.

"All you have to do is repeat a certain formula after me. But first, if you will excuse me, I must wash my hands."

Morgan opened a door and stepped inside a very small bathroom. He closed the door, and Maggie heard him turn on the water faucet. Over the sound of the running water she heard him talking to himself, chanting something. The water stopped splashing, and Morgan came back out, drying his hands on a paper towel. "Now then," he said, turning toward her and lifting both his hands, as if she were an orchestra and he was going to conduct. "Say after me: *I rise out of the egg in the hidden land.*"

"*I rise out of the egg in the hidden land.*" Maggie felt a wild desire to giggle.

"*May my mouth be given unto me that I may speak with it before the great god, the lord of the Underworld.*"

With prompting, Maggie repeated the bits and pieces of the spell.

"Now try this one. *Homage to you, oh ye lords of kas, ye lords of right and truth, infallible, who shall endure forever and shall exist through countless ages, grant that I may enter into your presence. I, even I, am pure and holy, and I have gotten power over the spells that are mine.*"

Maggie repeated the words. Her lips were beginning to go numb. "I don't like that one very much," she said. Her words were slurred and funny-sounding.

"Just one more. Try this one. *O ye great egg, ye shining disk, may I have the power of a servant and carry out all your wishes.*"

This is stupid, Maggie thought dimly, but just go along with it—otherwise you'll never find your way out. It's only words, anyhow. For safety's sake, she

crossed her fingers behind her back. She repeated
everything exactly as Seth Morgan said it.

"Very good! Excellent! Now then—uh-oh, who's
that?" Maggie heard voices coming toward them
through the basement. "Well, we're done. Let's go
back upstairs."

5

SETH MORGAN SHUT OFF THE OVER-
head light in a hurry. When he reached around the
corner of the bathroom to shut off that light as well,
Maggie caught a glimpse of a little figure on the
bathroom sink. It had curly hair and wore crumpled
jeans, just like Maggie herself.

Morgan hustled Maggie out of the wire door and
down the hallway, away from the voices. They hurried around corners and down strange hallways, always turning left, until finally they began to climb
a set of metal stairs. Maggie couldn't remember if she
had been here before or not. Then they walked
through a door, and there they were, right by the
Peruvian necklaces. Her father was standing in the
doorway of the mummy room, talking intently to
Julie. He ran over when he saw her. "Where have

you been? Julie was just telling me you went off with some stranger. I was about to call a guard."

"I got a special tour of the basement," said Maggie. "This man came up, and he said he was in charge of the Egyptian department, and so he showed me around. Wait—he was right here. Where did he go?" Morgan was nowhere in sight.

"You were in the basement?" said Maggie's father. "What happened? Are you all right?"

"She went through that door over there." Julie pointed across the gallery to the door marked STAFF ONLY. She looked as if she had been crying. "But when I tried to open it, it was locked. Then I didn't know what to do, because your father was gone, and there wasn't any guard around. So I just waited here."

"This Mr. Morgan showed me some Egyptian things, that was all." The words of the spell were boomeranging around in Maggie's head—*I rise out of the egg. . . . I, even I, am pure and holy . . . may I have the power of a servant . . . power of a servant . . . power of a servant. . . .* "Maybe we should go now. I still have to do homework!" Maggie heard herself sounding fakily cheerful.

"You just ran off and left me," said Julie. "I wanted to come, too."

"I was afraid he wouldn't wait," said Maggie, and she avoided looking Julie in the eye. A new crowd of children pushed past them and clustered around the mummies.

"Well, no harm done," said Mr. Jones, who was less inclined to fuss over danger than was Maggie's mother. He gave Julie a reassuring hug around the shoulders. "You did the right thing to wait here. Now what do you say we go home and take another look at that mummy?" No one remembered about going to the museum shop.

The rain had stopped. During the drive home, Maggie found it hard to pay attention to what Julie and her father were saying. As soon as they had parked, Mr. Jones bounded up the back steps and into the kitchen. "Looks like Maggie has found a mummy!" he announced to Maggie's mother. "There's one just like hers in the Egyptian collection."

"There is? Seriously?" said Mrs. Jones.

"Let's take another look at it. If it is a real mummy, I can't imagine how the O'Connells could have gotten their hands on it. Well, come to think of it, I can imagine."

"How can it be a mummy? It's so small," said Mrs. Jones.

"It's a kitten," said Maggie. "There were all these mummies—a bird and a dog and . . ."

"Don't tell me any more!"

"Maggie apparently met the curator of the collection," said Mr. Jones. "She says he showed her the storerooms in the basement."

"I even saw a mummy lying right out there on a table," said Maggie. "He said these Egyptian relics aren't so unusual."

Maggie's mother turned to her father. "What did you think of this fellow?"

"I didn't actually see him."

"I did," said Julie. "He looked like an absent-minded professor. I would have gone with them, but I couldn't get through the door. You should have waited for me, Maggie!"

Maggie's mother frowned. "You didn't have some sort of an incident, did you?"

Maggie shook her head. "No, no. He was perfectly okay, Mom, really."

"Bring down the mummy, Maggie," said her father. "We've got to be careful of it, if it's four thousand years old."

Maggie climbed the stairs reluctantly. She didn't want anyone to touch the mummy now, or even see it. She felt as if she had taken on a sacred trust. But when she reached her room, she saw that someone else had gotten there first. Minor looked up from the floor, where he cradled the partly chewed mummy between his paws. "Woof!" he said.

"Minor!" shouted Maggie.

Minor scrambled to his feet, picked the mummy up in his teeth, dropped it, picked it up again, and turned around, as if looking for a place to hide it. Maggie lunged forward and grabbed his collar. "Drop it," she said fiercely, putting her face close to his. Minor appeared to consider the idea. Then he whined and let the mummy fall from his teeth. The wrappings, partly torn, glistened with saliva. Maggie snatched it up and put an old T-shirt around it. Minor followed the little bundle with his eyes, his tail thumping on the floor. He was anxious to be back in Maggie's good graces.

"Bad dog!" she cried. She started down the stairs, holding the soggy mummy. "Minor got it—look!—it's wrecked!" She burst into tears as she lay the wounded treasure on the kitchen table.

"Goodness," said her father.

"Ugh," said her mother.

"Look at that," said Julie, leaning a little closer. "Its toenails are painted."

Maggie rubbed her eyes and peered through her blurry lashes. The tiny, shriveled object showing through the torn wrapping looked nothing like a kitten or anything else recognizable; it was a hard, dark, waxy wad, except for a pair of tiny paws folded over each other in front. Each paw had five gilded toes.

"It's painted with gold!" said Maggie's father. He took a clean dish towel out of the drawer and wrapped up the kitten. "We're going to put this well out of Minor's reach, and yours, too," he said to Spencer, who had just wandered in.

"Wait a minute," said Maggie. "It's mine. I was the one who bought it."

"When someone finds an ancient treasure, it doesn't really belong to that one person," said her father. "She's just the guardian." He carried the mummy into the dining room, opened the china cabinet, and put it up on the highest shelf. He closed the glass doors firmly. "We're going to keep it safe and out of harm's reach until we can take it in to the museum and let them decide if it's real or not."

Maggie and Julie sat on the floor in the living room for the next hour, supposedly doing Spanish and math. Maggie was smoldering. It doesn't belong to the museum, either, she kept thinking. As for where it did belong—Seth Morgan had entrusted her with its secret; he must have known she was exactly the right person to find out where the mummy came from and return it.

47

Maggie put down her pencil. A sense of possession seized her, giving her a warm feeling in her chest. So what, if her father said it didn't belong to her? She was the one to decide that, not him. The mummy wasn't out of her grasp yet. She looked casually through the living room door into the dining room. Nobody was anywhere near the cabinet. She could steal it back for herself and hide it for as long as she wanted. In fact, she could do anything at all with it. Her father hadn't made her promise to leave it there, and even if he had, so what? She didn't have to keep every promise. Even if she snuck it back to her room, that wasn't like stealing it, because it would still be in their house. And if it was stealing it, so what? She didn't have to obey every single thing her dad said, as if she were still six years old.

The more she thought about this, the more her mind went back to the museum basement. Find the tomb, he had said. She wondered what the rituals could be, and how she would know what to do. What if she herself could cast a spell? A tingle of excitement went up her spine. She wasn't going to mention this to her parents. No, the spells were going to stay Maggie's secret. The mummy, too—it had been her secret, and it was going to be her secret again.

Finally Julie called her mother, and finally Julie

left. Maggie could hardly wait to have the dining room to herself. That wouldn't be until tonight, though. She could hear Spencer and Tom in the kitchen, arguing over a cracker. They were such a pair of nuisances! She stepped over her unfinished homework and marched toward the kitchen. She'd tell them to pipe down, and she'd tell her parents the truth—that they were doing a rotten job with the boys. She startled Minor as she swept through the dining room. He jumped to his feet and did something he'd never done before—he growled at her: a low, hostile warning. His whole body was stiff.

"What's got into you?" said Maggie crossly.

Minor curled his lip and growled again. Then he seemed to forget about it. He gave a little whine, slurped his tongue once around his mouth, turned tail, and trotted off.

Maggie burst into the kitchen. "Can't you guys ever do anything but make noise? Can't you try to get along?"

They looked up in surprise, their faces smeared with chocolate milk and graham-cracker crumbs. "Ugh. Just filling up on sugar, are you?" Now Maggie's father looked up from the editorials section and gave her his Patient Inquiring Look.

"It's really your fault, Dad," she snapped. "You ought to be able to say no when they ask for all this

49

sugary stuff. What about their teeth? What about getting a sugar high?"

"What about it?" said her father.

Tom's and Spencer's mouths formed crumb-crusted O's. All three of them looked like such a cozy group, sitting lazily around the kitchen table in a comfy nest of comics and cracker boxes, that Maggie felt all the more annoyed.

"I'm just reminding you," she said. "It's what they tell us in school all the time. And can't you do something about that dumb dog? He growled at me. He's turning hostile or something."

"*He* is?" Her father put his pipe between his teeth, poked in some tobacco with his finger, and lit a match.

"You're going to give us all cancer with your stupid pipe," she finished.

A cloud of smoke gathered under the kitchen light.

"Anything else?" asked her father after a bit.

"I need to get out of here and get some fresh air," Maggie said abruptly. An odd excitement had come over her, as if all her energy had gathered itself to a fever pitch. Her ears were ringing, and her whole body felt supercharged. She grabbed her jacket from its hook by the back door.

"See you later," said her father mildly.

Maggie stormed out the back door. Just before she slammed it, she heard Spencer say, "What a witch." She flung open the garage door and wheeled out her bike. As she wobbled down the driveway, she glanced back over her shoulder. Her father stood in the lighted window, watching.

Good, thought Maggie. Give you something to worry about.

She hadn't thought about where she was going, but she found herself pedaling toward Chestnut Street. A witch—what did Spencer know about witches? Still, the idea made her unexpectedly uneasy. Witches had spells, peculiar powers, odd pets. She'd never heard of a child witch. It was sort of sudden, the way she'd gotten so mad at everybody. It wasn't like her usual self.

She stopped in front of the O'Connells' house and balanced on her bike, pushing herself back and forth with her toes. Nobody home. The house was dark. As she sat there, the thought came to her that the O'Connell boy would have to know where the kitten mummy had come from. She made up her mind that she was going to get to know him, even if her parents didn't like it.

She pushed off and rode to the end of the street,

51

turned right, went two blocks along Center Street, and turned onto Webster Road. It was very close to dark now, but she found she welcomed the shadows, the creeping darkness. It pleased her that she could steal along the edge of the street and scarcely be seen.

Mrs. Wilkins's house was the next-to-last one on Webster Road. Maggie hadn't realized she was heading here, either. The house was a fabulous ramble of stone and timber, with irregular niches and bay windows, a large stained-glass window facing west, and a cupola on top. Maggie wondered what she would see if she went up close and looked through the front porch windows.

There was no reason not to—it was just a house owned by a dead woman. She put down her bike and climbed the steps. The windows were curved glass and reflected the streetlight, but Maggie managed to peer through them. At first she couldn't see anything but stiff furniture arranged before a fireplace—no gold necklaces, no mummies. Then something caught her eye. On the floor by the sofa was a toy of some sort, the kind of thing a visiting grandchild might leave around. Only Mrs. Wilkins hadn't had any children or grandchildren; the newspaper had mentioned only her sister. Maggie pressed her forehead to the glass. It was a wooden pull-toy—she could see a bit of rope fastened to one end of it. It was a fat little hippopotamus on wheels.

She tried the front door handle. Locked. She hopped down the steps and went around to the back. A porch ran the width of the house, so it was going to be easy to reach one of the back windows. Maggie's head was buzzing with excitement. Seth Morgan had said something about royal children being buried with their toys. She had never tried anything like this, but she was sure she knew what to do. Still, the windows were set high in the wall; she'd have to find something to stand on. Maybe there was an old chair or bench in the yard. She stood at the porch rail and looked out into the shadowed lawn. Her eyes were getting so used to the dark that she could pick out all kinds of things, like a birdbath, and a rake lying under a bush, and someone's old boot—

"Who's there?" said a voice to Maggie's left.

Maggie's head cleared instantly. In the house next door a woman with white hair was looking fearfully out of a partly open window. It was one of the Harkness sisters. The woman couldn't see Maggie very well. Maggie didn't say a word, but slipped down the porch steps and strode around to the front and got back on her bike. Suddenly she was quaking so much that she could hardly get her foot on the pedal. The high-pitched excitement had gone. Something had made her come here, made her poke around the house. What in the world was she doing?

She tried to push off, half-falling in her panic, then gave up and ran for home, pushing her bike beside her.

6

"WE'RE READY TO EAT," SAID MAGGIE'S
mother, turning from a stoveful of steaming pots as
Maggie pounded through the back door. "Heavens,
where have you been?" Maggie grabbed the back of
a chair, as if that would keep her feet from carrying
her out again. "Are you all right?"

"I—I just rode home real fast," Maggie said between gasps. "Out of breath."

The good smell of pot roast filled the kitchen.
Maggie's mother handed her a big dish of noodles to
carry into the dining room. Her brothers were already at their places, wriggling with hunger. Maggie
sat down, and her mother began to serve the food.

"Feeling better?" Maggie's father inquired deli-
cately.

She had forgotten about stamping around the
house. "Guess I was in a bad mood," she said. "Just

55

grouchy." She shrugged her shoulders and tried to grin.

"Hormones," said her mother briskly.

"More noodles!" Spencer sang out. He waved his spoon, and the lone noodle still clinging to it flew off and stuck to the mirror over the sideboard. *"Noodles!"* He reached forward with his other hand and grabbed a fistful from the serving bowl.

"Spencer." Their mother fastened her fingers firmly around Spencer's wrist and guided his hand, noodles stringing from every finger, back over his plate. "Let go," she said.

"He's worse than Minor," said Maggie.

"Worse than Minor!" repeated Tom. "Slurp, slurp, slurp!" He made several dog noises, and his napkin and knife fell to the floor.

"Enough, Tom," said Mrs. Jones. "Could we please have Sunday manners this one day of the week?"

"This *is* Sunday manners," muttered Maggie.

"Sure!" said Tom. He leaned down to get his knife and napkin, then pretended to sit up straight and stiff, like a person in church.

"Could we change the subject?" said Maggie. "What do you think happens when someone dies?"

Her parents fell silent. A conversation stopper.

"I mean—do you think their soul lives on and goes to heaven? Or if they're dead, they're dead."

"That mummy's got you thinking, hmm?" said her father. "I say I don't know what happens. Many people believe the soul has a separate existence and survives and goes to heaven. Some people believe in reincarnation—you know, coming back as another person or animal. Most religions believe the soul is immortal. But I myself don't know."

"But what do you think probably happens?"

"I say the here-and-now is all I have time for," said Maggie's mother, sounding irritated. "We all have to die sometime. A long time ago, though, I read a story that has stuck with me. At the end of the story an old man dies. They happen to have weighed him right before his death, and then they weigh him afterward, and they discover a gap of a few ounces. So you can draw your own conclusions."

"I've drawn mine," said Mr. Jones.

"None of us really knows," said Mrs. Jones.

"You've never seen a ghost, though, have you?" asked Maggie.

"Never," said her mother firmly, "and I don't expect to. But speaking of the dead, Francie Gordon told me something odd. She said she'd heard that Mrs. Wilkins didn't die of a stroke or heart failure,

57

but of a poisonous bite of some sort, a spider or something. They couldn't figure out what bit her. She managed to call a cab to take her to the emergency room, but she was in a coma after that, and she died without waking up. Isn't that a shame? To live to be so old and then have something like that happen. Tom, what's under your plate?" She reached over and lifted the edge of Tom's plate, and there, tucked neatly out of sight, were five green beans. "You have to eat every one of those if you want some chocolate cake."

That night, as Maggie was getting ready for bed, she felt a surge of energy, and the high-pitched feeling came back. She was wide-awake. All she could think of was the cat mummy, lying at that moment between a glass pitcher and the carving board propped upright on its stand.

She dropped her underwear into her hamper and pulled on her pajamas, then ran downstairs to say good night. At first she couldn't find anyone. The bathroom was dark, the boys' room was dark, and there was nobody in the living room—just a wad of kid's underwear on the floor.

"Hey, Mom?" she called softly.

"Ssh," said a voice.

She saw something move inside Tom and Spen-

cer's room. Both of her parents were putting the
boys to bed. Some nights it was a one-on-one job.
That was all to the good: Maggie wouldn't have to
bother with them.

"Good night!" Maggie whispered into the dark.

"G'night," came the reply.

She hurried back upstairs, flicked off her light, and
jumped under the covers. It was only eight-thirty.
She set her alarm clock for eleven-thirty, in case she
fell asleep, but she was so keyed up she knew she
wouldn't need it.

She must have gone to sleep, though, and only
dreamed she was awake, because the next thing she
knew, her alarm was going off: little rings in bunches
of four. She grabbed the clock and pushed down the
button. Eleven-thirty. She listened, holding her
breath, hoping no one else had heard the alarm. The
only sound was the refrigerator humming in the
distance.

She got out of bed and crossed the room on her
bare feet. The floor was cold, but her bedroom slippers would make a scuffing sound. She inched down
the stairs, stopping between steps to cut down on the
creaking. She reached the bottom and was just
tiptoeing past the basement door when there was a
little rush of air, a whisking sound, and Minor came
pattering around the kitchen door. He stopped short

at Maggie's feet, stiffened, and growled low in his throat.

"Minor, what's the matter with you?" whispered Maggie. She patted him on the head, but instead of nuzzling under her palm the way he usually did, he froze, as if trying to decipher the touch of her hand. Then he backed away, his toenails clicking on the linoleum, and gave a short bark.

"Minor, you idiot, ssh!"

Minor growled again with even more conviction.

What had those words been? They came back to her with surprising ease. *"I rise out of the egg,"* she said in a low voice. *"I have gotten power over the spells that are mine. . . . Minor will not bark. My parents will not wake up."*

There, that was simple.

Minor continued to look at her as if she were a stranger. She didn't try to pat him again; he didn't bark, either. He stood attentively, watching her as she crossed the kitchen and went into the dining room. She opened the china cabinet doors. The bundle in the dish towel still rested on the top shelf. She picked up a dining room chair, carried it over to the cabinet, and climbed up on it. The top shelf was hard to reach, even with a chair, and it was tricky anyway, because the cabinet was crowded with things they never used—pickle dishes and wineglasses and porcelain soupspoons someone had brought them from China. She stood on tiptoe, reached carefully past the glass pitcher, and managed to capture the towel between her fingertips. She eased the bundle forward. She had almost gotten it to the edge of the shelf when a corner of the towel caught on the carving board stand and dragged it forward. It toppled off the shelf, smashed three plates, bounced off the counter, and crashed to the floor.

Maggie gasped, reached up on her toes, and grabbed the mummy. Her knees began to shake. She braced herself for her parents: They were going to come storming out here, their nightclothes flapping, and that would be that for Maggie and the mummy.

She waited, frozen on the chair.

A minute passed. No one came. How could they not have heard, spell or no spell? But someone had been wakened after all; someone was coming toward the dining room. Tom stumbled across the threshold, crying, "Mom? What made that noise? Daddy?" He stopped and looked up at Maggie.

Maggie jumped down off the chair, laid the mummy on the table, stepped over a piece of plate, and picked him up. "Never mind, Tomkins, it's okay. It's only me. Ssh, ssh!"

Tom howled, rubbing his eyes.

Maggie swayed back and forth to soothe him.

"Let's go back to bed, it's okay. Don't wake up Mom and Dad."

"Let me down!"

"Let's be real quiet," she whispered.

"Why did you break the plates?" His voice cracked with sleep.

"It was an accident. Ssh, ssh." Maggie made her voice as soothing as she could. "You're just having a dream. Time for night-night."

Tom let his head fall on her shoulder. She carried him back to bed and rolled him onto it. He burrowed without a word into the hollow beneath his quilt. Maggie pulled the covers snugly up around the back of his neck. In a moment he sighed, and then he was asleep.

The house was silent. Maggie crossed the hall and looked into her parents' bedroom. "Mom?" she said, not bothering to whisper. "Are you still asleep? Dad?"

Her parents didn't answer.

7

WHEN MAGGIE FIRST WOKE UP THE
next morning, she kept her eyes shut, trying to guess
if it was time to get up yet. Even with closed lids, she
thought the room seemed lighter than usual. She
turned over and curled up in a ball. The mummy was
safely tucked away in a shoe box in her closet. She
had picked up the pieces of the plates and stuffed
them down into the bottom of the trash can, which
had been fairly sickening, because then she'd had to
rearrange the garbage back over the plates to conceal
them. Then she had stuck three other small plates on
top of the pile in the china cabinet so it would be the
same height as before, and she'd wrapped the dish
towel around a small stuffed elephant and put that
back up on the shelf next to the carving board.

When she got home from school she was going to
take the mummy over to the Wilkins house and

somehow get inside, even if she had to break a window. She could use a quick spell to keep anyone from noticing the broken glass. She was already pretty good at spell casting—people always said she caught on to things fast.

She could hear her brothers squabbling in the kitchen, and somewhere in the background cartoon noises blared out. Cartoons? Wait a second. She sat up and looked at her clock. Nine-thirty. She should have been at school an hour ago.

Maggie jumped out of bed and scrambled downstairs. Tom and Spencer sat amid an assortment of cereal boxes and spoons and puddles of milk, staring at the television set. Minor looked up at Maggie from beneath the kitchen table, gloomy and silent.

"Where's Mom and Dad? It's late! I'm late for school!"

"They won't wake up," said Tom.

Maggie looked into her parents' bedroom. Two familiar lumps lay motionless under the quilt. "Mom! Dad! We're late! Get up!" Her mother turned halfway over, but didn't open her eyes. Maggie shook her father's shoulder. He snorted and pulled a pillow over his face. "Wake up!" she shouted. "Mom!" She shook her mother's shoulder frantically.

64

"Don't hurt her," said Tom. He was standing in the doorway, looking on.

"What'll we do?" said Maggie.

Tom shook his head and padded back to the kitchen.

Think, Maggie, think, she commanded herself. Seth Morgan hadn't taught her how to undo spells. What if her parents didn't wake up all day? Or ever?

"I rise out of the egg," she said slowly. *"I have gotten power over the spells that are mine. . . . Stop the spell. My parents will wake up. And Minor can bark again."* The exact moment she finished, Minor began to bark hysterically, as if he had been storing it up all night. Her mother and father sat up, then jumped out of bed.

"What's the matter with the dog?" said her mother.

"It's late—we've overslept by a mile!" said her father.

"Oooh. I feel awful," said her mother. "I've got a rotten headache."

Maggie's father made a face and rubbed his forehead. "I don't feel so great myself," he said.

Maggie dashed around getting ready. She couldn't find clean socks. She'd lost her homework, then found it where she'd left it yesterday afternoon, scattered all over the living room. She ate her breakfast standing up, slurping down a bowl of cornflakes in less than a minute; she forgot to pack a lunch.

"I'll need a note, Mom," Maggie said, "or Mrs. Garber'll send me home again."

"I don't know what happened to us," her mother kept repeating.

Maggie ran back upstairs for her backpack, but she couldn't resist stopping for a moment, her hand on her closet doorknob. She just wanted to take one quick peek. She opened the door. Her eyes traveled past the dusty shoes and fallen hangers to the shoe box, its lid securely on, resting on the floor. She noticed a movement on the closet pole, then a small, smiling face. Its eyes gleamed at her. . . .

Maggie jumped back. She shut the door with a bang and shoved a chair against it.

She was downstairs and nearly out the door when Tom came after her. "Did you tell about the plates?" he asked in a loud voice.

"I've got to go to school now. Let's talk about it after I get home." Maggie leaned down and whispered in his ear, "Don't tell. It'll be a secret just for us two."

"How come?" asked Tom.

"Let's go, Dad! Oh! My note!" Maggie took the folded piece of paper her mother held out for her and ran to the car, her backpack bumping on its straps.

On the way to school her father kept rubbing his eyes and saying he just couldn't seem to wake up. Maggie slid out of the car at the top of the hill. "What time is it now?" she asked.

"Ten-thirty."

"They'll just be going out for recess. Bye, Dad."

"Bye, dearie."

Julie's cubby was next to Maggie's, and she was standing there putting on her jacket when Maggie came into the classroom.

"Hey, you came after all!" she said.

"We overslept," Maggie explained.

Julie zipped her jacket and turned the collar up. "So when are you going to take it?" she asked.

"Take what?" Maggie pretended not to understand. She slowly slipped off her backpack.

"You know—the mummy. Or did your dog eat all of it?"

"Hey, Julie!" Alan Brown ran by, dodging in to yank Julie's ponytails.

"Stop it!" Julie tossed her head, and her cheeks turned pink.

Maggie busied herself rearranging stuff in the bottom of her cubby. She just wanted Julie to forget about the mummy. "My dad doesn't think it's the real thing anymore."

67

"How come?"

"He says it's something a kid made."

"He sure didn't think that yesterday!"

Maggie walked up to their teacher's desk to give her the note and turn in her half-done homework. "Our whole family overslept," she explained lamely.

"I see." Mrs. Garber sounded cool. She handed back the note. "Would you take this up to the front office, please?"

Maggie couldn't pay attention in social studies, and when the class went outside for afternoon recess, she didn't play soccer or hang out around the climbing bars the way she usually did; she just stood on the sidelines all by herself. She could hardly wait for school to be over.

Maggie's mother picked her up at three-thirty. "Are we going straight home?" Maggie asked.

"I've got to do a couple of errands, but they won't—"

"Errands?" Maggie squawked.

Her mother's eyes snapped. "You could always take the bus," she said. She looked closely at Maggie. "Your cheeks are bright red. Do you have a fever?"

"I feel fine!"

Maggie sat in the car twitching with impatience as her mother went in and out of the cleaners, the fish store, the drugstore.

When they finally got home, Maggie asked for the house keys, unlocked the back door herself, and darted upstairs to her room. Minor scrambled up the steps behind her, but she slammed the door in his face. She could hear him whining and scratching at the crack. She pulled the chair away from the closet door and slowly opened it. The *ba*-bird—she was sure that's what it was—was gone. She took out the shoe box and opened the lid. Still there. A tiny gold toenail gleamed in the half shadow of the closet. The mummy's round black eyes were calm and watchful.

"It won't be long now," she said to it. She emptied her school things out of her backpack, gently laid the mummy in, and zipped the pack up. She slipped it over her shoulders and started downstairs. Minor jumped up on her and nudged his nose against the backpack, knocking her into the wall. "Cut it out, you!" she said. She shoved away from him. He bristled and stood as still as stone.

"I'm going for a bike ride," she announced as she came into the kitchen. "I don't have any homework." Her mother was lifting out the garbage bag that lined the trash can. There was the unmistakable clank of broken plates. Maggie saw a sharp point of broken crockery poking through the bottom of the bag. She grabbed her jacket and raced out the door.

MAGGIE DIDN'T THINK ANYONE SAW
her push her bike behind the bushes next to Mrs.
Wilkins's house. She opened the gate into the backyard. It gave a raw scrape as it swung on half-torn
hinges. Patches of scraggly stems were everywhere,
remnants of summer weeds. The grass was colorless,
and the frost-killed flower beds were full of tangled
brown sticks and burst seed heads. The backs of all
the houses that overlooked the yard were screened
by tall trees. She couldn't see anyone, and no one,
she thought, could see her.

Then the grass behind her rustled, and she turned
her head. The O'Connell boy was standing there.
For a terrifying moment she was afraid she had con-
jured him up. A shock wave rolled through her, and
she swallowed and stared. He jammed his hands into

his jeans pockets and hunched up his shoulders. "What're you doing here?" he asked.

Her heart whammed against her chest. "What're *you* doing here?" she asked back.

His eyes scanned her face as if he were trying to read it. He was a lot taller than she was, and Maggie felt suddenly pressed down into a smaller size.

"The lady who lived here just died, you know," he said. He cracked his chewing gum. Maggie noticed he had a duffel bag slung over his shoulder. He set it on the ground. It looked empty. "I'm checking things out, making sure everything's okay."

"What's your name, anyway? Your first name?"

"Donnie. What's yours?"

"Maggie."

They both looked embarrassed.

"Have—have you ever been inside this place?" Maggie went on.

He shrugged. "Sure. Plenty of times. I used to do odd jobs for Mrs. Wilkins. How come?"

"You know that little statue I bought the other day? It's a mummy. A mummy of a cat, you know, from Egypt."

"That thing? Who said so?"

"My dad took me to the museum, and I saw one just like it. Exactly like it."

71

"Well, and so what?"

"So—I just wondered where you got it."

"You can go right on wondering."

"Is there Egyptian stuff inside here? There must be."

"Pretty nosy, aren't you?"

"There's supposed to be a whole Egyptian tomb that Professor Wilkins lost. Is it in there? Do you know?" She could tell from the look on his face that he did know. "I just want to look. I'm not going to take anything."

"Well, that's good. Sure wouldn't want you to take anything."

"Do you have a way to get in?"

He scratched his head and glanced all around him. "I haven't ever done this with a girl."

"Come on!"

"Well, you asked for it. Once you're in there, you know you're a criminal, don't you? Breaking and entering, that's a crime." He grabbed his duffel bag, took two big strides up the back porch steps, and began working at the bottom of the window. "Don't just stand there. You got to be fast. I'll go through first." The window scraped up. Donnie threw in his bag, hoisted himself to the height of the sill, and wriggled through. There was a crash. His face reap-

72

peared inside the window frame. "What are you waiting for?"

Maggie struggled to haul herself as high as the window. It was as tall as her chin, and there was nothing to stand on. She hooked one arm over the sill and scraped with her toes on the house wall. A car slowly passed the front of the house, and she could hear footsteps and voices approaching, coming up the sidewalk, people talking about a basketball game. Maggie froze until the voices were faint again, then gave a mighty heave and dragged herself through, landing with one shoulder in the kitchen sink. Somehow she twisted around and dropped to the floor.

She felt for the backpack straps and settled them on her shoulders, hoping she hadn't crushed the mummy when she rolled through.

"Okay, no rush now," said Donnie. He reached around her and pulled the window down.

The kitchen was appalling, even to Maggie's eyes, and she wasn't fussy. It looked as if no one had lived here for years. A thin layer of greasy dust covered the few sticks of furnishings—an ancient table with an oilcloth covering, two old wooden chairs with depressing little cushions tied on the seats, and a set of wilted curtains that drooped from a curtain rod on the back door.

73

"Stay away from the windows," said Donnie. He crossed the kitchen and opened a door to a passage lined with glassed-in cabinets and closed doors. Maggie followed him through the passageway to what must have been the main entrance hall of the house. It was paneled in dark wood, and high up on the walls she could see pale rectangles where pictures once had hung. A curved staircase led up past the stained-glass window to the second floor.

Maggie went across the hall and looked into the living room. There was the dark couch, smelling musty, but she didn't see the toy anywhere. It wasn't behind the couch, or at the other end.

"Hey, what are you doing?" said Donnie. "You got to keep away from the windows."

She ducked back into the inner hallway. "Just thought I saw something." She had seen it yesterday, she knew she had. Something very odd was going on here. If she did find this fellow's tomb, she was going to leave the mummy then and there and be done with all of this.

Donnie put his hand on her arm. "Now listen," he said. "Mrs. Wilkins never showed me this. I knew she had something hidden up here, but she pretended she didn't. When she went to the hospital, I thought I'd help her out, keep an eye on the place while she was gone. It was locked up, but I knew I could jimmy the kitchen window. I took a look around, and I just happened to pick up that little statue, whatever. You tell anybody about what's here, and it's yourself you'll get into trouble. Like I said, you're committing a crime right now."

Maggie nodded, and Donnie began to climb the staircase.

The musty smell was stronger on the second floor. The rooms were large and the hallway wide, but the house was dark. Donnie opened a door to a huge room with a dressing table and chairs and a four-poster bed covered with a sheet. A smell of ladies' powder clung to the room. "This was her bedroom," Donnie said, going in.

On the opposite side of the room Donnie opened another door, which led to a huge closet with built-in drawers and a full-length mirror and enough space to walk around in. Spiderwebs were thickly woven across the corners of the shelves, and when Maggie accidentally brushed a wooden ledge, her fingertips touched something thick and soft.

"Yuck!" She shook her hand.

Donnie stopped again. "You sure you want to do this?"

"I said I want to."

At the back of the closet a big zippered clothing bag of faded green plastic hung flat against the wall.

75

Donnie pushed the bag aside, revealing another door, narrower than the others. He pushed it open. "Look at what she hid in here."

Maggie stepped over knots of black dust and looked in. Only the dimmest daylight fell across the threshold. She could make out a narrow room with a tall ceiling. The walls were covered with scribbles, and right in the center, resting on a yellow stand, was a wooden box as long as a person. An eye was painted on the side of the box with strong black lines. In one corner of the room was a yellow chair, and a little table covered with objects was pushed against another wall.

"That's a coffin," Maggie whispered. She stopped. Her eyes must have adjusted to the dark, for at that moment she saw something move—something watery and pale, a fog that collected itself into a boy with a shaved head, naked to the waist. He took a step toward them, his mouth open as if he were struggling to say something; he stretched out smoky hands.

"What the . . . ?" said Donnie. "That thing wasn't here before." He began to back up.

The shape took another step. Donnie turned and ran. Maggie stood there as Donnie's footsteps got farther and farther away, until she couldn't hear them anymore.

9

THE APPARITION BEGAN TO SPEAK IN A child's thin voice. It sounded like gibberish at first, then formed itself into words. "I am Thutmose, King of Upper and Lower Egypt, son of the sun god Re. I am Horus the Hawk, and I have many other titles, too. I am fourteen years old and I died of a scorpion's sting."

Maggie had the awful pounding feeling she got when a bad dream began to repeat itself. "You sure d-do look dead," she whispered.

"And why not?" He also looked younger than fourteen—more like ten. He was hollow-cheeked and too thin, and he was a pale greenish color beneath his swarthy skin. He was wearing only a white skirt, a sort of pleated drape, and he was bare-chested except for a necklace as wide as a collar. The necklace was made of colored stones and gold. He went on talking. "This shape you see—this is my *ka*. You don't have to be afraid of it. This is what I looked like when I was alive. You have one, too, only you've never seen yours because you're not dead yet."

"Not dead yet?" Maggie whispered.

"I stayed with my corpse, naturally. Or, rather, my *ka* stayed. It's what everyone does till you get through the Underworld and arrive at the Fields of Reeds. And then you are restored to your full self. They say that happens, anyhow. If your body doesn't survive, if something happens to your mummy before you get there, then your soul is gone for good, and you are really dead once and for all. I was supposed to go through thousands of years ago, but I'm pharaoh, and I can do what I like."

"You stayed with your corpse?" Maggie couldn't help looking over at the wooden box. It was made of reddish wood and gleamed as if it had been polished.

"Yes, my mummy is in that coffin. That's only the plain outside box. Inside is the mummy case made for me, the most beautiful one ever created. It's shaped just to the size of my mummy and painted to look like me in all the regalia of the pharaoh. And inside the case is my mummy. That man Wilkins and his wife brought me to this room and set up my entire burial chamber. They found my tomb in Egypt and dug it up. The man died five years ago,

78

and now she's dead, too. You better be careful—a scorpion killed her, just like one killed me. It stung her right in this very room. There must be a nest in the house somewhere. Now, what are you doing with my cat? I want her back."

"How did you know I have her?"

"I saw you put her in that pouch you're wearing. I can go anywhere in my *ba*-bird shape. I've been in your room lots of times."

"So that was you!"

"I followed that boy, too. He's a grave robber. He'll be back, and what if he strips this whole chamber? You'll have to stop him. He has his plans, but he thinks he can fool you. Mrs. Wilkins always protected my burial chamber, but now you'll have to do it. You haven't told me your name. In my royal court you'd be put to death for refusing to give your name. Everyone would think you were an enemy."

"My name is Maggie Jones, and I am not your enemy. Or else why would I be bringing back your mummy?"

"I know that." He gave a little giggle. "I know everything, because I'm pharaoh, and I always will be. I've been here for forty years, which is longer than you've been alive. I've been here since your parents were babies."

79

"You've been in this closet for forty years? Aren't you tired of it?"

"I am not tired of it!" he snapped. "And furthermore, that's nothing compared with thousands of years in a tomb. Just wait till you try it. I wonder if you'll have a *ba*-bird after you're dead. I guess Mrs. Wilkins doesn't. I've been waiting for her ever since she died, but she still hasn't come back."

"Maybe only Egyptians have *ba*-birds," said Maggie.

"But we never finished what we were talking about!" He sounded fretful.

"Were you friends with her?"

"She was very fond of me. She drew all the hieroglyphics you see on the walls, and painted all the pictures." Maggie stepped over to the wall and peered at the birds and ovals and half-moons and fish; there was a crocodile and some men slaughtering an ox. She wished she had taken Morgan up on his offer and learned to read Egyptian writing.

"These pictures are everything I'm taking with me to the Afterlife," Thutmose said. "The pictures will turn into the real things once I get there. But Mrs. Wilkins brought me real offerings of food, too. See there, on that table? She said she wanted me to feel well taken care of."

On a plate at one side of the table Maggie saw an

ancient piece of bread and a bunch of tiny wrinkled grapes on a stiff stem. On the wall above hung a painting of a miniature door. The rest of the table was covered with a jumble of objects: a carved wooden boat with tiny human figures on board; bowls that gleamed like gold; a mirror; small statues of godlike creatures, some with animal heads. And there was the carved hippopotamus on wheels.

"I saw this downstairs, just yesterday!" Maggie exclaimed, picking up the toy.

"Don't touch that! You couldn't have seen it, because it has never been moved since the Wilkinses set up my burial chamber."

I did see it, though, thought Maggie. She put it back on the table. "Were all these in your tomb in Egypt?" she asked.

"Yes. When they first found the secret entrance, I thought they were tomb robbers and were going to destroy my mummy so they could get at the jewels and amulets. I was terrified when they began to take everything apart. But they packed it all up safely into trunks and boxes and carried it with them on a boat across the ocean. While we were on the boat, I heard Mrs. Wilkins talking about me, about how I had been so young to be the ruler of all Egypt, and I decided to let her know I was there. That's when I found out that your people don't expect to see spirits.

81

"Professor Wilkins ran in when he heard her scream, and then he became very excited, because he had always wanted to study the Egyptian belief in life after death, and this was the best chance he would ever have. So they agreed to pretend that my burial chamber had been lost in shipping, and they would secretly set it up just as it had been in Egypt. I promised I would tell them everything I could remember about Egyptian religion and Egyptian life. Mrs. Wilkins asked me lots of questions about my life in Egypt and about how I died."

Maggie was getting used to Thutmose's peculiar, whining voice. She lowered the backpack onto the floor. "It must have been kind of lonely here," she said.

"I had the Wilkinses. And my *ba*-bird could always fly outside. At the end of each day Mrs. Wilkins would ask me where I had been, and she would explain what I had seen. I used to watch children playing behind a school—sometimes they threw a ball through an orange hoop, and Mrs. Wilkins told me what that was. Sometimes I followed them home and listened to their families talking. And I flew everywhere else—to grand cities, over forests and lakes, into caves hidden far beneath the earth.

"Then Mrs. Wilkins began saying I ought to make my journey through the Underworld, and not wait

82

any longer. She said she knew that as long as she was alive, she could protect my mummy, but once she had died, she couldn't be sure. I asked her if she was ill, and she said no, but she was getting old. Then one day she told me that she had decided to go to the museum and tell them about my tomb, and the next day she was stung. The last thing she said to me was that I must go."

"So why didn't you?" asked Maggie.

"I just don't want to yet. That's what they all said, the other spirits I met after I died—go on through, you're an innocent child, you won't have a moment's trouble. And once you're past the Hall of Judgment, you will go to the Fields of Reeds and find your parents again."

"Don't you want to see your parents again?" Maggie started to slide down to the floor, where she could sit comfortably, but she remembered the nest of scorpions and jumped back up.

"I do, but later. My mother and father died when I was a baby, and I had only my uncle to bring me up. My uncle was father and mother to me. He was my father's younger brother—and a magician!"

"I just met someone who knows about Egyptian magic," Maggie interrupted.

"My uncle was greater than that, whoever it is. He was going to teach me to be a magician, too, when

I was older. He could cure dog bites and infections. He could change his own shape so he looked like someone else, or make you think you saw something that wasn't there. He was the most powerful magician of his time. He said I would need to know magic when I was the sole ruler and people would try to trick me or be jealous of me and try to seize my power. He was going to teach me everything about defending myself with magic. But it was all for nothing."

"What happened?"

"I died. I was stung at night. While I was asleep, a scorpion crawled onto me and stung me on the neck. That's the worst place—neck stings kill you the fastest. It hurt a lot. I woke up screaming, and the spot swelled up, and I got a terrible fever. Then I began to have dreams. I dreamed my whole body was swollen, and my skin turned dark and purplish as the poison flowed everywhere, and my tongue swelled up and turned black, and I couldn't breathe—then I was looking down on myself, and I could feel everything I was suffering, but I was apart from it, too. And then I died. It took three days for me to die. That's how long it takes a scorpion's sting to kill a child, three days. My uncle Set was raving with worry and grief, but there was nothing he could do. When I died, my *ka* was released, and it stayed

84

with me while my body was prepared by the embalmers. I lay in the embalmers' tent for sixty days, with natron salt piled over me. First they cut out my internal organs, and they took out my brain through my nose—"

"Eeww!" Maggie cried out. "Don't tell me!"

"It isn't the slightest bit terrible once you are dead. And their knives are sharp and accurate—they know just how to make the cuts. They take out your liver and your lungs and your stomach and your intestines, all the important things, and each of your organs gets preserved in its own special jar. There are mine, in that square chest. Your heart stays in your body, though. Then after sixty days, you're done, and you get a big burial procession. They did a beautiful job with me, or so everyone said. I had the very best perfumes and salts, and I am wrapped in the most exquisitely woven linens with scarabs tucked in everywhere, jewels wound in with my shroud cloths, because of course I am the pharaoh."

Maggie suddenly knew she was going to be sick. Maybe it was the stale air in the dark closet or the powdery smell that clung to the dead woman's bedroom.

"Still," the whining voice went on, "you're so thin when your mummy is done. I used to be strong—I was a very good runner. I don't think I could run a

85

single step now. Are you good at running? Some of my cousins were good, the girls, I mean. Sometimes I met them at my grandmother's."

"I better go home," Maggie said in a trembling voice. She'd give him his cat and get out of here. She hoped he wouldn't mind the tooth marks.

"You can't go!" he said.

"I don't feel too good."

"But you have to put my cat in the coffin with me. And I want you to talk to me some more. The Wilkins woman always used to talk to me."

"Not right now." An awful picture had come into Maggie's head. She saw herself dragging a small bandaged shape that was Thutmose's mummy over to a window and throwing it out, so that it smashed to the ground below. The scene was so vivid she had to look down at her own arms and legs to be sure she wasn't actually doing it. Her throat got hot and dry, and an urgent nausea was moving up her throat. She began to see little blinking points of light, and her stomach gave a dangerous lurch. She scooped up the backpack and dropped it at the boy's feet.

"Wait!" he cried, suddenly frantic. "Don't leave me all alone! You have to come back! Say you will! Promise me!"

"I will," choked Maggie. She darted from the

room and stumbled down the stairs, swallowing and clenching her teeth.

She reached the front door and fumbled with the bolt. As she wrenched the door open and burst out onto the porch, she remembered—too late—why she and Donnie had gone in the kitchen window. The Harkness sisters, next door, were starting up the steps of their front porch, their arms full of grocery bags.

"What are you doing there?" one of them called to her. She sounded frightened.

Maggie ran from Mrs. Wilkins's house as fast as she could go. She glanced back once over her shoulder and saw the two women talking to each other and looking in her direction. She thought of putting a spell on them, to make them forget they had seen her, but she was too flustered to remember how to do it right. She ran home at top speed, gulping in the cold air until her stomach felt all right again.

10

"IS SOMETHING CHASING YOU?" ASKED her mother as Maggie hurtled into the kitchen. "This is the second day in a row you've come racing in here like you were doing the hundred-yard dash."

Maggie wanted to walk around the kitchen and kiss her mother, grab a dish towel, pat the cabinets, anything just to make sure she was back in the real world. She reached down and rubbed her cheek against Minor's smooth, doggy-smelling fur.

Had she really just been talking to a ghost? She had always hoped she'd be able to see a ghost, but she hadn't really expected it to happen. Maybe this wasn't a regular supernatural ghost but was more of a scientific type of one. She remembered how Seth Morgan had said the *ka* was a form of the human spirit that stayed in the tomb. Maybe *ba*-birds and *ka*s had existed only for Egyptians, and then had become extinct. Scientists were always discovering new rays and forces in the universe, laser beams and "emissions." Maybe Thutmose was a historical emission that had collected itself all in one place.

"Maggie, are you listening?" Her mother sounded exasperated.

But what about that vision she'd had of herself destroying Thutmose's mummy? What had come over her? She wondered if leaving the kitten mummy counted as completing the tomb. She had a feeling it didn't. She wished she could ask Morgan a few more things. Maybe there were parts to this spell he didn't know about.

"Think I'll go upstairs and do my homework," she said in a fake good-girl's voice.

"You didn't hear a word I said!" exclaimed her mother. "I thought you didn't have any homework."

"I meant hardly any."

"Oh." Her mother's nod was skeptical.

Maggie went upstairs and sat cross-legged in the center of her bed and spread out her math papers. *Two trains were going at different speeds. . . .*

The strangeness was beginning to slip away. What did it feel like to be a ghost? Did you get hungry or tired? For that matter, what had it felt like to be an alive Egyptian? All those times she'd seen pictures of them standing sideways—now she had a

89

chance to find out what else they did. Thutmose had kind of a revolting personality, but what would you expect if you'd been stuck in a closet for forty years? In spite of what he'd said, his loneliness must be awful.

Her math papers slid to the floor. As soon as she could, she was going back to the Wilkins house. She knew how to get in. She could get a spell ready to use on the Harkness sisters, though they looked awfully frail. Even if they did see her, they probably couldn't do much but cluck and scold. She had told Thutmose she'd be back, and she was not going to leave him there waiting for her.

Now that she had decided, she felt a faint buzz of excitement start up again.

Maggie picked at her supper, even though it was her favorite, cheeseburgers and Greek salad. She especially loved the salty Greek olives. She tried to avoid looking Tom in the eye, but she knew sooner or later he would say something, and he did: "Hey, Maggie, what about the plates?" Luckily, his mouth was full, and nobody else understood him.

"If you can keep a secret, I'll give you a surprise after supper," she said. "But don't say anything more about you-know-what. *Not anything.*"

He nodded.

"What you-know-what?" asked Spencer.

"Nothing," said Maggie.

"But you said about a you-know-what!"

"You wouldn't be interested," said Maggie.

"I *am* in'erested." He kicked his chair.

"Oh, Spencer," sighed Mrs. Jones. "Just let them be."

After they had finished eating, Mr. Jones crumpled up his napkin, walked over to the china cabinet door, and turned the knob.

"You're not getting it out again, are you?" said Maggie's mother. "It's so gruesome!"

"All right," said her father, taking his hand off the knob. "I was just going to check on it. I thought Maggie and I could take it to the museum next weekend and let them examine it."

"Want me to clear the table?" said Maggie, jumping up to distract them. She gathered up her plate and Tom's and rattled their silverware all together on top.

"Are we through?" asked her mother.

Maggie whisked away the salad bowl. "Tom's going to help me," she said. Tom slid halfway down from his chair. "Bring the napkins, Tom," Maggie commanded. When he obediently brought a fistful of crumpled paper napkins out to the kitchen, she leaned over and whispered, "Wait here, I'll be back in a minute." She darted upstairs, got a wrinkled paper bag from her closet shelf, returned to the kitchen, and led Tom down the hall to his room.

"I'm giving you the surprise," she said in a low voice, "but only if you promise not to tell anything about last night. I was doing something important, and I don't want Mom and Dad to know about it. I'm going to tell them later. If they find out, something awful might happen." She watched Tom's reaction. "Something awful could happen to me or Mom or Dad—or you." His eyes got wide and dark. She didn't want to scare him too much. "But everything will be fine if you don't talk about it."

"What if I forget?"

"That's what the surprise is for. Every time you think of it and you're afraid you're going to tell, just take a piece of this." She opened the paper bag. It held all her leftover Halloween and Valentine and Easter candy. Some of it was more than a year old, but Tom wasn't fussy. "We'll put it—let's see, somewhere where Spencer won't get into it, and Mom won't find it. How about behind these blocks?" She made a hollow space at the back of the stack of cardboard blocks, stuffed the bag into it, and replaced the blocks to cover it up. "There!"

"Okay!" Tom clapped his hands.

"But remember, *don't tell.* If you do, I'll take it all back. Now I'm going to go help clean up."

Maggie was carrying dishes out to the kitchen when the telephone rang. Her mother answered it, then kept glancing at Maggie while she was talking. "Well," she said as she hung up. "We need to have a talk, it seems."

"What about?"

"That was Edna Harkness, over on Webster Road, next door to Mrs. Wilkins's. Late this afternoon she and her sister saw a girl run out of the Wilkins house, and the girl looked like you. And it seems that earlier there had been a boy in the Wilkins yard with her. Miss Harkness says he looked like one of the O'Connell boys."

Maggie shook her head. "Wasn't me."

"They were sure the girl was you."

"Maybe their eyesight is going. They're both over eighty, Mom."

"Maggie, this is serious. If you were over there, and if you were in that house, we have to know it. You don't realize how much trouble you can get into."

"Well, do you believe me or them?"

"I don't know who to believe. *Whom,* I should say." Her mother looked her right in the eye. Maggie

93

was silently squirming. Don't tell, she commanded herself. She had often envied kids who could cheerfully tell a lie now and then. She had never been able to do it without worrying half to death afterward.

"Mom, I am not going around breaking into houses."

"I also was talking to Peg Prentice yesterday—she hears about everything on Parker Hill—and she says the younger O'Connell boy isn't leaving town. After his parents move, he's going to live with an aunt till the end of the school year. Is that who was in the Wilkins yard? Are you getting to be friends with him?"

"Not really." At least that was true. Maggie made herself meet her mother's eyes while keeping an innocent expression on her face. She couldn't stop a blush from spreading up from her collar, though. In a moment her face was pounding, roasting-hot red. The very skin on her face felt self-conscious. When she blinked, her eyelids sort of stuck together.

Her mother didn't say anything while the blush came to a peak. "I know I can trust you to tell me the truth," she said finally, and she left the kitchen. Maggie slowly finished sponging off the counters.

Two hours later, Maggie remembered her bike. She had left it leaning against Mrs. Wilkins's house.

94

She couldn't tell her mother, but she couldn't leave it there, either; someone would be sure to steal it. Her father was sitting in the living room smoking his pipe and reading the *Wall Street Journal.*

"Dad?" Maggie said softly. "I left my bike outside. Will you come with me to get it?"

"Can't you go out by yourself?"

"It's a ways up the street."

"Well, that's not a good place for it." He sighed and put down the newspaper. "Okay, let's go."

They put on their jackets and stepped out into the chilly night air. When they had gone a few yards, Maggie said, "Actually, I left it over by Mrs. Wilkins's house."

"What were you doing there?"

"Just looking around."

They walked the rest of the way without talking. Cold autumn smells filled the air—damp earth, piles of raked leaves. In the clear black sky Maggie could see a few icy-white stars. As they approached Mrs. Wilkins's driveway, some small nocturnal animal scuttled away from Maggie's feet. She pushed aside the bushes and pulled out her bike.

"At least nobody stole it," she said. She stood with her father and looked into the backyard, stretching away into darkness. She heard a faint scratching that reminded her of something, she couldn't think what—a persistent sound, like insects on a summer night.

Suddenly she wanted badly to tell her father about Thutmose, and about Donnie showing her how to break into the house, and about the words she had repeated in the museum basement and now she wished she hadn't. The darkness seemed to grow and press upon her; she could barely make out the stalks of dead summer flowers, scraps of things formerly alive, their shapes suggested in the black depths of the yard. There was a world in the dark out here, one about to stir with its own life, and she was afraid to say anything, afraid even to describe one part of it, standing next to her peaceful, reasonable father.

"Shall we go?" he said. Maggie pushed her bike home in silence.

11

THE NEXT MORNING MAGGIE MADE
sure she had plenty of dimes in her pocket. There
was a pay phone in the front hall at school, and they
were allowed to use it at recess. Julie was waiting for
her by the coat hooks.

"Hey, are you upset about something?" she asked
Maggie.

Maggie pushed some books into her cubby and
took out her spelling folder. "I don't know."

"Are you mad?"

"Gosh, no."

Julie had already collected her homework and a
geography book and three new pencils, freshly
sharpened. Maggie could smell the wood shavings.

"Are we still friends?" Julie asked.

Before Maggie could answer, Penelope Miller
came up to Julie and stood close to her, while keep-

97

ing an eye on Maggie. Penelope had been trying to be best friends with Julie for over a year, but Julie and Maggie had always been first-best friends.

"See you later, I guess." Julie walked slowly away, with Penelope practically leaning on her shoulder.

Wait a second, thought Maggie. But the thought didn't make it into words.

When the bell rang for morning recess, Maggie darted from her desk, her hand clenched around two dimes. Julie was right behind her. "Are you coming out?"

"In a minute. I've got a phone call to make."

"I'll come with you."

"No. *No.* Go away. This is private."

Maggie saw Julie's face close up, and Julie walked away. Maggie took the telephone book from the shelf and looked for "Museum of Fine Arts." She dropped in her dime, dialed the number, and listened through a recorded message. She hated making phone calls to adults she didn't know, and she practiced what she was going to say in a whisper. "Could I speak to the mummy room?" she said when the operator came on the line.

"I'll connect you with the Egyptian—" Some clicks followed, then a woman's voice answered: "Egyptian department."

"Could I speak with Mr. Morgan?"

"Who?"

"Mr. Morgan. Seth Morgan."

"Do you have the right department?"

"He's in charge of Egyptian things, like scrolls and mummies."

"No, dear, I'm afraid not. That's John Fox. You must want some other department."

"But he showed me the mummy in the basement."

"I don't know about that. Let me check the directory. Let's see—K, L, M—Morgan. . . . No, no one is listed here with that name. Why don't you try the Children's Museum? Maybe you've got it a little mixed up."

The woman hung up. Maggie stared at the phone. Could she have made a mistake about his name? Could he have said John Fox and she thought he said Seth Morgan?

At lunchtime Julie gave Maggie a look across the cafeteria and sat down next to Penelope. They both took out their lunches. Maggie went over to their table. "Can I sit here, too?"

"I guess," Julie said with a shrug. Penelope didn't say anything. Maggie took her sandwich out of her lunch bag, then an apple, and finally a packet of cookies.

"Maggie's got a mummy," Julie said coolly to Penelope.

"A mummy? A mommy? Oh, you mean one of those dead Egyptian things? What for?"

"It's not a real one," Maggie said.

"One time my aunt found a fossil," said Penelope. "A huge fossil, I mean—a whole animal, just pressed into stone. It was real. She was on a dig." Penelope got up and brushed crumbs off her sweatshirt. "I'll be back in a minute. Don't let anybody take this place, okay?" She headed for the bathroom.

"After we finish, let's go outside for a walk, over by the hill," said Maggie in a low voice. "I have to ask you something about the mummy."

"*What* mummy?" Julie said. "You just said it wasn't real."

Penelope came back to her seat, and her smile faded as she scanned their faces. "You've been talking about doing something, haven't you?" she said. "I can tell."

Neither Maggie nor Julie answered. In a moment Penelope gathered up her lunch bag and wrappers and milk carton and went away.

Maggie and Julie finished eating in silence. Then they put their trash in the wastebasket and walked out to the farthest corner of the school yard, a place where some swing sets faced the side of a hill, and they could climb a little way up the hill and sit and talk without anyone hearing them. They settled themselves beside a flat boulder. A cold wind blew through the brown grass.

"I know I've been acting sort of funny lately," said Maggie. "The mummy *is* real. Not only that, it belongs to a pharaoh, and I found *his* mummy, and also, his spirit is still around."

Julie drew back. "What?"

"His spirit, you know—his ghost."

"Where did you see it? It didn't come into your room, did it?"

"Well, actually—well, the mummy's in the Wilkins house, that big house near ours. It's where the dead archaeologist used to live."

"You were in their house?"

"I climbed in the kitchen window. This boy helped me, the one I bought the mummy from at the yard sale. Actually, my parents told me he used to break into houses."

"Maggie! Have you gone crazy?"

"There's a hidden room like a closet that's been made into a burial chamber, and that's where the spirit is."

Julie didn't say anything.

"Do you believe me?" Maggie stopped. "You don't, do you."

"Well, what do you expect?"

"Do you remember that man at the museum, the

one who took me down to the basement? What was his name? Was it John Fox?" Maggie was whispering now, for no reason, since the playground was deserted. Everybody else was playing soccer in the sports field. She had been staring down the street as she talked, toward the dead end, where a few triple-decker houses were clustered, when she saw a figure on the other side of the school's cyclone fence. She hadn't noticed him walking up; he just appeared there, wearing a brown cloak. Then he turned toward them, and she recognized Seth Morgan, not wearing a brown cloak at all, but the same clothes he had worn in the museum, and looking nearsighted, just as he had before, with his glasses sliding down his nose and his stomach paunching over his belt. She jumped to her feet and started down the hill. "It's him, Julie! Come on!"

"I don't think you should," said Julie.

Maggie kept on. He must have known she had tried to call him and somehow figured out where she was. "I found the burial chamber that my mummy belongs to," she said as she reached the fence.

"*Your* mummy?" He frowned. "It doesn't belong to you."

He looked different this time: He was even more disheveled than before, and his eyes were rimmed with red, and he had a funny smell, like dirty socks.

Maggie felt a growing uneasiness, even on this side of the fence, with the wire diamonds between them.

"Um . . . right. No . . . it doesn't . . . I mean the one I found. I tried to call you at the museum, but they hadn't ever heard of you."

"I'm only a part-time curator, and they can never keep track of the part-time people. They probably put you on to Fox, did they?"

"That's who they thought I wanted. But let me tell you what happened. I found the tomb—and there's a ghost in it."

Morgan didn't seem surprised. "You didn't talk to him, did you?"

"Yes, I did, but the strangest thing was—"

"I should have warned you. Never talk to apparitions. Never. It can be very dangerous."

"He didn't seem dangerous to me, just lonesome. But something stranger happened. I think a spell got ahold of me and tried to make me destroy his mummy."

Morgan cleared his throat three times and looked up and down, everywhere except right at Maggie. He looked pretty uncomfortable. "I must explain to you," he said. "My powers are small, and I learned them only after years of diligent study; their source is a great magician of ancient times. I probably never should have taught you anything—you are too

103

young. But you seemed to have a natural aptitude. That's the way it is with magic—either you have it or you don't."

"What do you mean?"

"I wish I could help you, but I can't. The scrolls tell about this boy king, that his spirit refused to go on his Underworld journey—he was cowardly, you see, and kept upsetting the natural order of things. It seems that you really have been charged with completing his tomb. And your charge involves more than that. You must carry the task through, whatever it may be. If it means destroying the mummy, then that is what you must do. Of course the museum would be unhappy, but they don't ever have to know."

"That's what I'm supposed to do? That's what those spells were for?"

"If you don't do it, something will happen to you, or your family."

"I don't want to do it. I've changed my mind."

"You can't. Once you've said you will complete a sacred task, there's no escape."

"Why? Why does his mummy have to be destroyed?"

Morgan ignored her question and leaned close to the fence. "You don't need to be afraid. The boy is actually dead, you realize, and has been for eons.

There's nothing much to the mummy by now. Just a bundle of bones and dust, wrapped in rotten linen. It's terribly fragile. It will disintegrate as soon as it touches the air."

The awful smell coming from Morgan grew worse, as if something disgusting was leaking from every pore. He moved away, giving her a contemptuous glance over his shoulder.

"You can keep your stupid spells!" she called to his retreating figure. She turned to walk back toward Julie, but Julie was no longer there. Maggie could see her in the distance, walking in the school door. The door closed behind her, and Maggie was left to cross the empty school yard alone.

12

THAT NIGHT MAGGIE KEPT WAKING UP
with bad dreams. She heard a boy crying, and then
she was standing with a lot of people beside an open
grave, and they were all murmuring, "Where is he?"
and Maggie was trying to conceal a heap of white
fragments by stuffing them into her backpack. The
trees in the cemetery were full of dark birds with
smiling human faces.

She felt awful in the morning. She looked awful,
too, as she saw in the bathroom mirror—pasty-faced
and puffy-eyed. She stumbled down to the kitchen.

"Are you coming down with something?" asked
her mother when she caught sight of Maggie.

"I don't know. I had a bad dream."

"That can happen when you're starting to get
sick."

"I was awake all night."

106

Her mother pressed her hand to Maggie's forehead. "You're not feverish, but you look like you need to stay home today. You'll be better off in bed if you feel that bad."

Maggie ate a piece of toast and crept back upstairs. Kitchen noises drifted up the stairwell. She heard her father leave. She heard Tom's voice, then Spencer's, then her mother talking to them, and the clink of bowls and plates, the scrape of chairs. She curled up under her quilt and closed her eyes.

The dream had been waiting for her. The same sick feeling came back, and she was trying again to hide the white fragments, only they wouldn't fit, they kept spilling out, and they looked like pieces of bone. . . . She sat up with a gasp of fright and shook her head. She was going back to see Thutmose, no matter what, but she wasn't going to destroy his mummy.

Her mother called to her from the back hall, "I'm going out for a while—I'll take the boys and lock the door. Don't bother answering the phone. You just stay in bed and get plenty of rest."

"Okay."

Her mother was going out. Once again Maggie's blood started to hum, and the high-pitched excitement of the spell came surging back full-force.

Her mother called up again from the foot of the stairs. "Do you want me to get you a video?"

"Sure. How about *Parenthood?*" Maggie's voice sounded perfectly normal.

"How many times have you seen that?"

"*Police Academy,* then."

"I'll see what they've got."

Maggie could hear the boys getting their jackets zipped, and then they were bundled out onto the porch. Her mother pulled the back door shut. Silence. Maggie hopped out of bed. Who cared about school or homework or even bad dreams? It all slid away from her as easily as if she had tipped a roomful of dollhouse furniture to one side. She would go back to the Wilkins house now and talk to Thutmose as much as she pleased, and put the cat mummy where it was supposed to be, and she could use a spell to make sure her mother didn't come home too soon.

"I rise out of the egg. I have gotten power over the spells that are mine," she said out loud. A feeling of confidence swept over her. *"My mother will keep on shopping and doing errands until I come back."* Then she pulled on some clothes, ran downstairs, and took the spare key from the hook. When Minor came grumbling up to her, she brushed him forcefully away with her leg—it was really a long, slow kick—and went out the back door. She locked the door, shoved the key into her jeans pocket, walked quickly

down the driveway. There was no point in taking a chance on her bike being seen.

She took the long way around to Webster Road so she could stay out of view of the Harknesses' house. As she was coming up the sidewalk, though, she saw a familiar jacket.

"Going back in?" said Donnie.

"What's it to you?" Maggie replied.

He walked along beside her. She speeded up.

"Where're you going?" he asked.

"I don't have to tell you. Why aren't you in school, anyway?"

"Why aren't you in school yourself? You going back inside? Even with that thing in there?"

"Why not? Doesn't scare me."

"Hey—are you okay?"

"Of course I'm okay."

"You look a little wired."

"You leave me alone or I'll tell my parents. They could get you into trouble. You've been in trouble before, haven't you?" She knew the threat would catch him by surprise. They were right in front of the Wilkins house now. She turned on her heel and walked rapidly away, up the Wilkins driveway and onto the back porch. She'd have to take the chance that the Harkness sisters weren't watching out their window at that moment. Anyway, what if they were? She pushed the window up and slid across the sill. Nothing to it. Then she leaned across the sink and closed the kitchen window and locked it. Donnie's face, looking confused, appeared briefly in the glass.

Up the central staircase and through the empty bedroom, the dressing room, and the door—still standing open—Maggie hurried to the hidden chamber. She couldn't imagine why she had felt sick before.

There was her backpack, right where she had dropped it on the floor. But where was Thutmose? Nobody home? She had no idea how to find a spirit. It seemed stupid to look under the coffin stand, but she checked anyhow. Then, with a shrill whoop, something brushed her shoulder and whirled past her up into the corner of the chamber.

"Just joking!" crowed Thutmose in his *ba*-bird shape. He poised himself in the high corner, drew up his feathers, then dive-bombed Maggie. She squealed and ducked, and the *ba*-bird vanished and a pale, boy-sized blur gathered like a fog at the side of the coffin. "Back again!" he said as he materialized. He stretched out his skinny hands, his complaining face cracked in a smile. "You came back!" he said. "Just as you promised. Now give me back my cat."

Maggie bent over, unzipped the backpack, and took out the mummy. "I'm afraid our dog got ahold of it, but he only chewed through the wrappings." She held it out by one corner to show him.

"She's all right. I already know that." A small, silvery shadow leaped from the corner of the room into Thutmose's arms. The kitten had glowing green eyes and short, perky ears. It rubbed its whiskers with one stubby paw as Thutmose kneaded the back of its head.

"So that's who you were!" said Maggie, leaning forward to pat the animal. It dissolved under her hand, a swirl of cold mist.

"She'll be back," said Thutmose. "Now put her mummy into the coffin. She belongs there. Her body has been prepared just like mine. We'll stay together for all eternity."

"You mean take off the lid?" Prickles danced across Maggie's shoulders. What was really in there? The mummies she had seen at the museum were neat and dry and perfect, but there was no telling what they had looked like when the museum people first pried off the lids. "I'm . . . just . . . I really don't want to. I'm not used to the idea the way you would be."

"Do as I say!"

"Do it yourself!"

"How stupid can anyone be? I can't."

111

"Why not? Just because you're a pharaoh?"

"It's impossible. I don't have a body. A *ka* must persuade living people to do things for him."

"Well, can you wait a minute?" Maggie set the kitten mummy down on the table with the gold toys and shriveled food offerings. She picked up the hippopotamus on wheels. "Did you really play with this?"

"My parents gave it to me when I was a baby. My grandmother told me that when I was learning to walk, I dragged it around with me everywhere, all through the palace and the courtyards and outside in the sun, and even slept with it under my bed."

Maggie laid it back in its place. "When you have your kitten's mummy back with you, are you going to go on your Underworld journey?"

"Maybe."

"What if something happens to your mummy before you go?" She was beginning to feel uneasy stirrings. "This house could catch on fire, it could be struck by lightning, a robber could break in. What are you waiting for?"

"How would you like it if you had to go through the Underworld all by yourself? You have to go past terrible things. One evil man has the pivot of a great door fixed in his eye. You can hear him scream each time the door is opened. Others braid ropes of straw till their fingers bleed—but they can never finish, because donkeys stand just behind them eating the ropes as they are made. And others are starving for food, and they keep reaching for bread and jugs of water, but whenever they come close, demons dig pits at their feet, and they slip down with nothing, and have to start over again."

Maggie gulped. "But if you hadn't done anything bad yourself, couldn't you go by without them noticing?"

"There are lakes of fire and monsters everywhere, and pits full of reptiles, each with seven heads and their bodies covered with scorpions, and serpents with teeth like iron stakes that will crush you, or part of you, like your head. And besides that, all through the Underworld are gates guarded by monster gods, and you have to know each one's secret name in order to pass by—like Faceless One, Wallower in Slime, Feeder on Carrion.

"And after that, you still have to answer questions in the Hall of Judgment. Ammit waits right underneath the scales where your heart is being weighed. You can't see her, but you can smell her and hear her teeth grinding, and she's stupid, too. If you make a mistake in your answers and they throw your heart down to her, you can't talk her out of eating it."

"Even if it was just a mistake?"

"That's what the scrolls are for—so you won't make mistakes. My uncle made sure I knew all the rituals and steps of getting through to the Afterlife. And if he had finished teaching me his magic, too, I would know for sure that I could get through. Magicians always know the right things to say, even when they aren't telling the truth. My grandmother said a powerful magician could get away with almost anything. But she said the heart of a murderer always betrays itself."

"When did she say that?"

"Lots of times. She lived in a small house near the palace, and they let me visit her once in a while. She didn't get along with my uncle. She was my mother's mother. She fixed me herb drinks and fruit drinks to strengthen me, and let me play with her little tortoise. She gave me my cat." The kitten reappeared, starting with its nose, by Thutmose's chair. It hopped up onto his lap, yawned, and rubbed its ear with its paw.

"Sometimes she told me to be wary of my uncle— that he was ambitious. But I told her what he told me—that he was so talented, he would have made a wonderful pharaoh himself, if only he had been born the eldest, instead of my father. When I told her that, she looked surprised and said I was to take care, that I was the one true pharaoh, and I must never forget that. She told me about my great ancestors and said that if I did everything just as the priests said, and went to school, I, too, would be a great pharaoh. I did my best—but I was hardly ruler at all. It would have been better if I had never been born."

"Don't say that!"

"But I never got to do anything brave or show my powers. My uncle did, though, because he got to be pharaoh after me."

"He must have been very upset when you died."

"At least he made sure I was buried in a magnificent tomb. I still wish I knew how it happened. In Egypt we have lots of scorpions, and people have special wands made of hippopotamus ivory that they put near their beds at night to keep scorpions away. Somehow this one scorpion got past my wand and onto my headrest."

"Maybe someone moved the wand."

"You mean on purpose?"

Maggie's heart jumped to hear the words. She shouldn't have said that.

"If someone let the scorpion in, that's murder," said Thutmose. "If I knew for sure, I would tell the gods in the Hall of Judgment. Then that person's soul would be devoured and destroyed forever. The pharaoh is sacred. He's not like other people. No one can kill the pharaoh!" Thutmose's voice dropped.

"My uncle knew who my enemies were and kept them away. He got rid of the ones who lived in the palace. He found them out, one by one, and soon there was only my uncle and me and a few servants living with us."

"Maybe there was just one that never got found out," said Maggie.

"That's what Mrs. Wilkins said. She said she had been studying the scrolls and she thought someone had been jealous of my power and had wanted to kill me for it. She said she had an idea who it could have been, but she died right after she told me. She was probably wrong, don't you think?"

"Who'd she say it was?"

"Well"—his voice wavered—"she said it was my uncle."

Maggie felt a peculiar tension mounting in her body, so that she felt all jumpy and tight. An odd atmosphere permeated the dark little chamber, something urgent and grim. She felt an impulse: Someone else was about to move her hand and make her lift the coffin lid.

Thutmose went on, whispering half to himself: "But it *couldn't* have been my uncle. He wouldn't have, I know that. My grandmother used to say the perils and sorrows of a ruler were many. I used to wonder if she was trying to tell me something without saying it out loud. She gave me a warm embrace each time I had to leave her, and she gave me an amulet to wear for protection against evil. But it wasn't strong enough to keep away the scorpion."

The high-pitched feeling was back, making Maggie's face hot and her whole head hum—she couldn't hear anything over the roaring in her ears. She walked over to the coffin and lifted off the lid. Thutmose stopped talking. He clutched the ghostly kitten to his chest. Maggie felt numb, as if she were encased in clear plastic. She watched her hands reach down and touch something smooth. Nestled in the coffin was a beautiful mummy case, painted in turquoise and brown and gold and green, a swath of painted feathers covering its shoulders, a face looking up with sad yet tranquil eyes. She was going to lift this mummy case out and drag it to the bedroom window and hurl it to the ground, where it would shatter.

"You're not putting my cat in," whispered Thutmose. Maggie saw his eyes open wide with fear. "What are you doing? No! Don't!"

Maggie had lifted the mummy case up to the rim of the wooden coffin. She couldn't say anything. If only she had been able to speak, she'd have told Thutmose that she couldn't stop herself. As she tilted it toward the floor, Thutmose darted around trying to hold her back. She felt breaths of cold smoke

117

13

MAGGIE SCREAMED AS DONNIE BURST across the threshold. "You scared me half to death!" she yelled.

Her scream rattled Donnie, too. "What are you doing up here? Who were you talking to? Is that ghost thing still here?"

"He's gone. I don't know where."

"What's that on the floor?" He stared into the mummy's painted eyes.

"It's the mummy case. I dropped it."

"Is this what was in that box?"

"Yes. The actual mummy is inside. Something tried to make me throw it out the window."

What if the spell came back yet another time? She had been turned into some sort of living shawabti. "Someone has power over me, like remote control. He's making me do things I don't want to do."

"I never saw a ghost till the other day," said Donnie, "but I know enough not to fool around with the dead."

"That ghost was only a boy pharaoh named Thutmose. What you saw was his *ka,* and that's his spirit looking like he did when he was alive. He also flies around in the shape of a bird with a human head."

Donnie muttered something.

"You remember I told you about going to the museum?" Maggie said. "A man was there who knew about Egyptian things—his name was Seth Morgan—and he told me to take the cat mummy back to the pharaoh's tomb. He taught me some magic spells to help me find the tomb, but he also put a spell on me. And now he says I have to destroy the mummy."

"What for?"

"I don't know. He just says it's in the scrolls."

"Nobody can make you do things if you don't want to do them."

"He's got magic power, though. He got it from an ancient magician."

"You think it's like black magic?"

"What's that?"

"Magic that does evil. You hear about it sometimes. Maybe you need a priest to exorcise it."

"I don't know any priests."

Donnie scratched his head. "Maybe the spells aren't real—could be he's got you hypnotized."

"They're real. I put a spell on my own mother this morning."

"Show me one."

"Put a spell on you?"

"Sure."

"I don't always know how they're going to come out."

"Try it."

"Okay, but you may not like it." She repeated the formula and then said: *"You're going to jump backward."* Donnie's feet flew out. An invisible hand took him by the back of the neck and tossed him across the narrow room and slammed him into a wall. He crumpled into a heap on the floor.

"I'm sorry! I told you!" Maggie rattled off the words to end the spell. "See what I mean? Are you all right?"

Donnie pushed himself to his feet. His face was white, and he rubbed the back of his head where it had hit.

"I guess so." He looked pretty shaky.

"Ssh—what's that noise?" They held themselves still. A faint rustling and scratching came from somewhere close by. "This place has mice, or rats," whispered Maggie. "We better put the mummy back in

121

the coffin." She was afraid the spell would come back over her as her fingers touched the mummy case, but nothing happened. How light and small it was! Its eyes looked up and out, but not quite at them, as they laid it back in its outer coffin. Maggie picked up the cat mummy from the table and tucked it in, then she and Donnie gently replaced the wooden lid.

"Let's get out of here," said Donnie, suddenly panicked.

Maggie snatched up her empty backpack, and they ran from the burial chamber through Mrs. Wilkins's bedroom and down the staircase. Donnie stopped Maggie in the kitchen. "If it's black magic, you've got to get rid of it. My aunt's real religious. Want me to have her ask the priest?"

"It's got to be someone who knows Egyptian magic."

Somewhere above them a floorboard creaked. Maggie froze in front of the kitchen window. What if Morgan found someone else to destroy the mummy? It was easy enough to get into the house. Or he could put an even stronger spell on Maggie, one she couldn't shake off. Mrs. Wilkins had wanted to tell the museum about the tomb, only she had died before she could do it. Now it was up to Maggie to get the mummy out of there and into safekeeping.

"If we went to the museum," said Maggie, "we

could find the real curator and tell him what's here. They'd have to come get it, wouldn't they?"

"Beats me. Can they do that if it isn't theirs?"

"Morgan said they'd been looking for it for years." She stopped as another, worse thought came to her. "Oh, no! What if he's at the museum, too?"

"You've got your spells."

"I never tried one on him. You come with me. I don't know how to get there by myself."

"It's easy. The thirty-nine bus goes right by it."

"Come with me, *please*, Donnie. You have to. You've seen the ghost, too."

"Maybe. I'll call you. You think your mom will have a fit if it's me on the phone?"

"Oh! My mom! I forgot! I've got to go home! I'll meet you at Davis's Drugstore tomorrow when I get home from school."

A couple of minutes later, she was standing by her own back door fitting the key into the lock. She opened the door, hung up the key, and a moment later her mother pulled up in the driveway. Maggie looked out the kitchen window. Her brothers were practically buried beneath grocery bags and shopping bags. The entire car was full.

Her mother was surprised to see her up and dressed. "You know what the rule is," she said. "You have to stay in bed if you're home from school. You really do look pale. Why don't you get a quilt and lie down on the couch? I picked up some videos you'll like, and some for the boys, too."

She went out again and reached through the back door of the car and unfastened Tom's and Spencer's seat belts and then came back in with two plastic bags crammed with videos. "Mom!" said Maggie. It would take days to watch them all. Her mother didn't seem to notice that it was an unusual amount. Tom and Spencer came in, chortling to each other. Mrs. Jones went out again and began bringing in bag after bag of groceries. The first two were filled with packages of cookies: Oreos, chocolate middles, vanilla wafers, chocolate-striped chocolate, marshmallow sandwiches—it looked like one of everything the store had on its shelves. Then came a grocery bag full of packages of potato chips and corn chips. Then bottles of apple juice and cranberry juice. Then six-packs of orange and lemon-lime soda. Tom and Spencer were hugging each other and crowing and pointing as their mother lined up the bags on the kitchen table.

"She went ape!" sang Tom. "Everything we said we want one of she got! She put it in the basket!"

Mrs. Jones was now lugging in bags of hamburger meat and hamburger rolls and hot dogs and hot-dog rolls and pickles and mustard and catsup.

"Can we have cookies?" Tom practically shouted. He was dancing around in circles, beside himself with excitement. He stood on his tiptoes, reached for a package of Oreos, sat down on the floor, and started to tear off the cellophane.

"Tom!" called their mother in a suddenly different tone of voice. She was shouldering through the back door with the last pair of grocery bags. She put them on the counter, shoving the others back toward the wall, and then surveyed the scene before her as if seeing it for the first time.

"Those are for dessert," she said slowly, and took the torn-open package from Tom's hand. She stared at what she had collected. "How could I have spent all that money?"

Maggie stole a glance at the grocery slip her mother was holding. It was a yard long, and the purple print at the bottom said $300.23. Her mother shook her head. "I've never done this in my life—just spent money without thinking. And on junk! I had been saving that money for—oh, never mind. We must have been there for an hour and a half. And these videos—whatever went through my mind?"

Maggie tried to laugh.

"I want a cookie!" said Tom indignantly. He had watched the riches being heaped unbelievably into the grocery cart, and he wasn't about to take no for an answer. "You promised!"

"I did? I don't remember. Oh, well—okay. Have some milk, too." Maggie's mother put three Oreos in a stack by Tom's place at the table and two beside Spencer's. She poured them each a glass of milk. "When you're done, why don't you watch a video with Maggie?" she said.

Maggie took *The Flintstones* out of the plastic bag and went to the study, where the big television set was, and put the tape into the VCR. Tom and Spencer came along a moment later, licking chocolate crumbs off their fingers. They settled themselves before the television set. As Maggie was about to shut the study door, she caught sight of her mother, still standing in the kitchen, and to her horror she saw that her mother was crying. She was standing all alone, not making any noise, and her face was crumpled up, as if she weren't a grown-up anymore.

Maggie felt sick. She curled up into a miserable ball in the corner of the couch and pushed the play button.

Later that day Maggie's mother put the boxes of cookies in the basement freezer and lined up the bags of chips and popcorn in the back of the tool closet. She told the children they'd just think of it as their year's supply of junk food. But Maggie heard her discuss it with her father when he came home, and she sounded plenty worried. "I wonder if I should make a doctor's appointment," she was saying. "You know what's scary? I can hardly remember being at the store. And the other night—the night you took away that mummy thing from Maggie—I had a terrible night, I had very strange dreams, and the next day I felt like I had a hangover. There was this cloud in my head all day."

Maggie's father said a doctor's appointment probably would be a good idea.

"You mean in case it's something physical—some real problem," Maggie's mother said slowly.

"Just to make sure that it isn't."

"You mean something wrong with my brain."

Maggie wished she could explain it all to her mother, tell her it was only a spell and not a terrible disease, but things had gone too far for rational explanation. And who was to say it was "only" a spell?

Her mother scarcely touched her food at supper time. Maggie's father leaned over the table and said in a hearty tone, "Not to worry. Everyone has their off days. I had one myself, that same day. We all overslept, remember?"

Maggie's mother frowned. "Maybe we have some kind of pollution in the house. What does radon do

127

to you? I'm going to take some aspirin and go to bed early."

"Want me to clear the table?" offered Maggie. "I'm feeling a lot better. I think I'm over whatever it was."

"Thanks," said her dad.

Maggie cleared the table and put the plates and glasses into the dishwasher and rinsed every single fork carefully, something she usually didn't do. What if she had permanently harmed her mother? There could be parts to the spell she didn't know about, things hidden in the hieroglyphs.

That made one more reason why she had to get to the museum. Even if the real curator, Mr. Fox, wasn't interested in magic, he could read the scrolls and tell her how to undo spells.

14

MAGGIE WAS HOPING DONNIE WOULD
call her the next morning before school, but when he
didn't she decided not to take any chances. *"I rise out
of the egg. . . ."* she began as she pulled her sweatshirt
over her head. *"Donnie will meet me at the drugstore
today, so we can go to the museum."* Right away she
felt better. By sundown, or by tomorrow at the latest,
Thutmose's mummy was going to be safe. She pictured Mr. Fox, whoever he was, amazed at her discovery. She had no doubt that he would believe
her—all he'd have to do is come see for himself.

Julie didn't talk to Maggie when they were standing by their cubbies getting out their school things,
and she didn't even look at her during recess. Maggie
wondered if it was going to be impossible to get back
to being best friends again.

When she got home from school, her mother offered her some store-bought cookies and milk, but Maggie managed to eat only one.

"I'm going up to Davis's for shampoo," she said in a careless voice.

"Fine," said her mother. "Take a five-dollar bill from my wallet. My purse is on that chair."

Maggie found the money, and then, so her mother wouldn't worry, she muttered a small spell: *"My family will not notice I am gone."*

"See you later!" she said, and set off up Parker Street.

If her spell hadn't reached Donnie and he didn't come, she had made up her mind to go by herself. The bus stop was across from Davis's. Maggie had taken the 39 bus before. It went to the central library downtown, and there was a stop marked MUSEUM halfway along. She felt for the change in her pocket, quarters and dimes, as she hurried toward the corner.

He was there. He was waiting for her by Davis's plate-glass window. It was after four o'clock by now, and growing dark.

"I was afraid you might not come," she said. "I put a spell on you. Did you notice?"

"Take it off! I don't want one of them on me."

"It's used up by now."

"Ask me first next time. I was going to come anyhow."

130

They crossed the street.

"It's the thirty-nine bus, isn't it?" said Maggie, trying to get back on friendly terms.

"Right."

"It'll only take us a few minutes to get there, won't it?"

"Right."

All the public transportation stops were marked with a big T. A small crowd waited beneath the sign in the blue twilight. Behind them, the Mexican restaurant was starting to get busy. The ice-cream parlor had turned on its neon ice-cream cone in the window, and Maggie could smell hot pizza at the Friendly Eating Place, the sub shop on the corner. She caught Donnie's eye and grinned with nervous excitement. Then the door of the sub shop opened, and a man walked out and behind him came a dog, tall and square-headed, mostly yellowish white, a dog of unreal size, a giant dog, with huge, sturdy legs and big feet and a mean jaw. The dog came straight for Donnie and gave a snarling growl that rose to loud barks. "Jeez, what have I done?" said Donnie, sticking his hands in his pockets and stepping backward. The dog advanced, stuck its nose at Maggie's knee, braced itself, and barked again. It bared its teeth. Maggie backed away. The dog wasn't interested in any of the other people waiting for the bus, and, oddly, they didn't notice the dog. Donnie and Maggie were being pushed toward the plate glass of the storefronts. Then the dog stood on its hind legs and tried to put its paws on Donnie's jacket, but he shoved it away and turned his back. "Get out of here!" he shouted.

The bus was coming toward the stop now—Maggie glimpsed its tall, square form slowly bearing through the traffic. As it pulled up to the sign with wheezing brakes, the crowd gathered and pushed toward the curb. The dog, suddenly, was gone. Maggie felt in her pocket for quarters, but as she got close to the bus, she saw that the bus routes must have been changed again. The sign on the front said 72—HUNTER'S POINT rather than the familiar 39—COPLEY SQUARE. She and Donnie stopped as the crowd surged around them and pushed aboard. The bus lumbered off with a rich roar of exhaust.

Maggie and Donnie waited alone beneath the T sign. Almost right away, another bus appeared in the traffic, this time with the right sign—39. It was empty. It pulled up and stopped just for them. Maggie dropped in her fare. The driver didn't even look at her. The doors slapped shut and the bus pulled away as soon as Donnie got his foot on the bottom step. They staggered to the first row of seats. The driver seemed to be going awfully fast—the bus swayed and lurched and they were thrown forward as it stopped short at an intersection. Maggie looked out. There was the animal hospital, set back on a hill. Nobody got on the bus. The driver closed the doors and took off. Maggie couldn't remember ever seeing the next stop, and the one after that looked unfamiliar, too. Maybe her view had always been blocked by people standing in the aisles. But no one got on at either place, and the bus stayed empty except for the driver, who ignored them, his face hidden by his cap, his two-way radio blatting out unintelligible bursts of noise.

"Where are we?" Maggie asked Donnie.

Rows of brick apartments with crumbling entrances, a liquor store with a grate over its display window, a string of houses set close to the street—why did it all look different?

"Should we get off here?" she asked Donnie.

"I don't know where this guy is taking us," he said in a low voice.

Now they were swaying along a nondescript city street, past curving rows of low apartment buildings. Donnie buzzed to get off. The bus stopped at a corner by a yellow T sign. Two ladies with bulging plastic grocery bags got on, and Donnie and Maggie slipped away into the darkness. As the bus went down the street, Maggie saw that the number on the back was 148.

"How'd we get on the wrong bus?" she said.

"I don't know. I've never been here before. And there isn't any one forty-eight bus that I ever heard of."

"Are we near the museum?"

"We're not near anything."

A tilting cyclone fence by the sidewalk blocked off an empty field. Across the field, in the distance, were lights and buildings and the comforting sound of traffic. On the other side of the street was an abandoned school, its windows boarded up, its steps cracked and full of weeds. From around the corner of the school trotted a large yellow dog—no, thought Maggie, it isn't possible: the same dog as before. It came toward them, barking and growling.

"Don't move," said Donnie.

They stood stiff and still. The dog stopped a couple of feet away and looked at them, as if deciding what to do. Maggie thought she saw a man in the shadows of the torn school fence, but it was only a trick of the twilight.

"Walk slow," said Donnie.

Maggie put one foot in front of the other as deliberately as if she were walking a tightrope. After several yards of silence, she turned back to look. The dog was gone. They were standing on a broken sidewalk in a wasteland of torn-down buildings, mysterious sheds and shacks, old truck bodies, and a few men wrapped in ragged coats who concealed their faces and faded away into the shadows. The dark had closed around them, though the sky in the west was still blue above the horizon and a few thin clouds caught the gold brilliance of the setting sun.

"The museum is nowhere around here," said Maggie.

"Who cares about the museum! How do we get home?" said Donnie. "There's no street signs around here." They picked their way up the sidewalk, but they were forced to stop at the next corner, which was flooded with dark water and glistened with green oil. Something stirred below the surface of the water.

"Don't step in that!" cried Maggie. "Let's try to cross up there." She pointed to the right, where the sidewalk led to dry ground. A gust of cold wind came up behind them, pushing them along and stinging their backs. Tiny pellets of ice whirled momentarily in the air. Maggie wrapped her arms around herself and hunched over. They passed someone

135

slumped beside a huge cardboard box; he looked dead, until Maggie saw one of his eyes, open and alert, watching her as she passed.

"Watch it," Donnie hissed, putting his arm out to stop her. They had started to cross at the next corner when a boy in a satin jacket appeared, walking toward them with slow, deliberate steps. Two more boys were behind him, and two more came up from the right, and then more gathered out of the air, it seemed—melting into sight, and bearing down on Maggie and Donnie. "Don't set them off," muttered Donnie. The gang ranged before them, halting them in their tracks. Maggie could hear their jackets rustling, and she saw small, tight smiles on some of their faces.

"This here's a dead-end street," said one of the boys. "You can't go no further."

15

THEY HAD SPREAD OUT, BLOCKING THE
way. Donnie motioned for Maggie to stay back.

"Easy now," he said. He relaxed his stance, so he
looked as if he was on guard, but not challenging
them.

The silence stretched out. One or two of the boys
shifted their feet and stuck their hands in their pockets and raised their shoulders so they seemed to grow
larger in their jackets. They kept taking a few steps
forward, moving closer. Off to one side something
gleamed in the dim light, but Maggie didn't dare
turn her head to see what it was.

"Just passing through," said Donnie. His voice
sounded perfectly steady, and his legs weren't shaking the way Maggie's were.

"Tell me about it," said the boy in front. His blond

hair was cut flat on top and letters were shaved into the sides. "Tell me all about it."

"Nothing to tell," said Donnie.

There was a clinking noise, and one of the boys toward the back took out a length of chain from his pocket and whirled it by one end. Then he poured it back and forth from one hand to the other.

"We're going around," said Donnie with deliberate calm. He motioned for Maggie to follow him, and they turned to the left, walking slowly away from the paved street. "Don't look back," Donnie muttered. Maggie wanted to run, but instead they crept along, stumbling down a dirt path, away from the distant lights of civilization. Weeds grew thickly on either side, weeds that had trapped bits of trash, cardboard boxes, paper wrappers.

Nobody seemed to be following them.

"Why aren't there any people here?" Maggie whispered.

"Some kind of no-man's-land, maybe where they tore down stuff for the toll road, only the road never got built."

A billboard, most of its enormous sign torn away, stood atop a dark building. The scrap that remained had something written on it, something that caught Maggie's eye—drawings of eyes and birds and peaked lines. A long piece of paper like a banner blew up from the weed-infested gutter and wound itself around Maggie's ankle. She stopped to tear it away and saw more drawings filling it in long columns. White graffiti, scrawled across the back of a brick building, glowed in the dark.

"Do you know where we are?" asked Maggie.

"Nope. Just keep walking. West is that way, so south is over there, and that's heading out of the city. So if we walk toward the west, we'll have to get back to Parker Hill. Try a spell again—find out where we are. Try one now."

Maggie cleared her throat and closed her eyes and concentrated. *"I rise out of the egg. . . . Show us where we are."* She opened her eyes a crack. She was hoping to see scruffy old Center Street again, or a sooty 39 bus, or the sub shop. Nothing changed at first. Then the landscape seemed to deepen, and into the distance stretched a wilderness in which she perceived dim human forms, some of them moving slowly under great burdens, some of them strewn across the ground, barely crawling. A pair of scrawny arms reached up from a kneeling form, then the body fell into some hidden chasm. A snake as thick as a tree rose from the chasm, its flat-nosed head twisting all around, as if looking for someone, and

139

then another head darted up beside the first, and then a cluster of snake heads sprouted beside that one and began to bob and weave.

"Make it change," said Donnie urgently. "Change it back to where we were."

Maggie's teeth were chattering. "*I . . . have . . . gotten . . . power. . . . Change everything back to where we were.*"

Nothing happened.

"I can't do it," said Maggie. "The spell isn't strong enough."

Someone was shouting in the distance, so far away they couldn't make out the words. It was a terrible shouting, like that of someone in agony: over and over again, the same scream floating to them from somewhere.

"Let's get out of here!" Maggie clutched at Donnie's arm. "We don't know where we are or what's going to come after us." They began to run blindly, stumbling over curbs and broken cement, cutting across abandoned yards, pushing through shoulder-high weeds, shoving through an old iron gate that swung free behind them with a tooth-shattering screech. "Which way did you say was west?"

"Where the sun goes down, over there."

Maggie looked up, toward the incongruous crimson and gold strip of sky that lay beneath the encroaching dark of night, and she thought she saw something—a bird with black wings, perched for a moment on a low tree branch. Then it was gone.

"Did you see that?" said Donnie. "Did you see its head?"

"Go that way." Maggie pointed toward the place where the *ba*-bird had disappeared.

They broke into a run. A brick wall came into view, and behind it the back fence of the animal hospital, and then the sign at the bus stop. They were only three blocks from Maggie's house. As they stood on the corner, a 39 bus rumbled past them, loaded with people coming out of the city after work.

"We made it!" said Donnie. "We made it out of there!"

"I'm going home," said Maggie. She was even more scared now—it had all caught up with her, and her knees and legs were shaking like mad.

"Wait a second—what happened? Where were we?"

"It looked like the Egyptian Underworld, the way Thutmose described it."

"The Underworld?" said Donnie. "You mean the Egyptian hell?"

"That's pretty much it. Yes."

"How did we get there?"

141

"It must have been Seth Morgan. I told you those spells were powerful. He doesn't want us to get to the museum. He doesn't want the real curator to know about the tomb."

"Morgan's the one who told you to wreck the mummy?"

Maggie nodded.

"So why don't you do it?"

She hadn't thought of that. Why shouldn't she let Thutmose look out for his own fate? He'd had plenty of chances to save himself—she couldn't help it if he still refused to go. She would just put his miserable tale out of her head. She wouldn't think about him and his pull-toy and waking up at night with a scorpion on his neck. What could she do for him, anyway? As Morgan had pointed out, he was dead.

But she could still hear his spirit pleading with her to stay and keep him company. "It would mean his soul is dead forever," she said to Donnie. "Think what it would be like to do it with his ghost right there, going crazy, begging you not to."

"So it's sort of like murder."

Maggie nodded.

"Why is it so important to Morgan? What does he care?"

"I don't know."

A skinny black cat came out of the shadows by the

supermarket and wound itself around Maggie's ankles. She pushed it gently away. It yowled and began to rub its back against a tree trunk.

"How come Morgan doesn't do it himself?" asked Donnie.

"He didn't say why." Maggie looked at the cat, now rolling over and over in a scruffy patch of weeds by the base of the tree. "Maybe it's like Thutmose. Thutmose can't do things for himself, because he's a spirit."

"Maybe Morgan is some kind of spirit, too."

"I want to go home *now*," Maggie said abruptly. She was feeling more quaky every minute. "But give me your phone number in case I need to talk to you. So I won't have to use a spell."

Donnie wrote out his aunt's number on a gum wrapper, and she folded it into her jeans pocket.

As she came up her street, Maggie noticed that the sunset was still in the sky. It seemed to have been there an awfully long time, and when she walked in the back door she saw that the kitchen clock had scarcely moved while she was gone. It was still four forty-five. Her mother was sorting laundry on the dining room table, Tom and Spencer were shouting at each other in the basement, Minor was deep in sleep, his paws twitching as he dreamed.

Maggie climbed the stairs to her room and shut the door.

"Maggie, it's meat loaf—I thought you would love it," said her mother.

Maggie looked at her plate and shook her head. "I'm not very hungry," she whispered.

"She just needs the catsup," joked her father, putting the giant red bottle in front of her place.

Maggie shook her head again. She was about to say to him, Dad, I have to tell you something. I took the mummy over to Mrs. Wilkins's house, and there's a lost tomb in her attic—but he probably wouldn't believe her. And if he did, and they went to the house, what if some other spell came over them?

Minor was under the table scavenging for crumbs, and his head suddenly appeared by Maggie's knee, the tablecloth draped over his ears. He plopped his head down on her leg and whimpered and looked up at her with pleading eyes.

The telephone rang. Mr. Jones got up to answer it.

"Someone selling aluminum siding," he said as he came back to the table.

In a moment it rang again. Mr. Jones sighed, got up, and answered it. "No, thanks, we're not interested."

He settled himself in his chair, and it rang a third time. Maggie got up to answer it.

"Hello?"

"I must remind you of what you promised to do." Maggie recognized Morgan's smooth voice, though he didn't bother to identify himself.

"I don't want to do it anymore. I told you."

"Soon you will be eager to do your job."

"I won't!"

"You'll see."

The line went dead.

"Was that Julie?" asked Maggie's mother.

"Nope. Somebody else."

"From school? Have you and Julie had a fight?"

"She doesn't want to talk to me."

Mrs. Jones gave her husband a significant look. "You've been acting so strange lately, Maggie. Is something going on we should know about? I promise I won't be mad, whatever it is."

Maggie just shook her head.

After supper Maggie stood at the kitchen window, looking across her backyard and the neighbors' yards to the Wilkins house, an immense shape that defined a block of darkness. Purple streetlights shone around it, and a couple of tall hemlocks made one shaggy black edge. She thought she saw someone moving in

145

her backyard; then a person walked across the patch of grass and shadows by the garage. Maggie blinked. She might have seen pale sleeves, a varsity jacket. Could it be Donnie? She couldn't see anything more, unless there was a dark place in the shadows, a place darker than the rest.

Maggie looked over at the kitchen wastebasket. "Want me to take out the trash?" she asked, pulling on her jacket.

"Do we need to?" asked her father, glancing into the trash bag, which was only half full.

"There's something kind of . . . *whiffy* in there," said Maggie. She twisted the top of the trash bag closed and took it outside. She crossed the driveway and looked cautiously around the corner of the garage. "Donnie?" she called. She couldn't see very well. Two ailanthus trees cast sharp shadows through the purplish light from the street lamp down the block. Donnie stepped out from behind the back wall of the garage. For a moment Maggie remembered the strange sensation she'd had at the museum, that someone threatening was close at hand. Maggie could see her father come into the kitchen and look around, just as he had the other night. In another minute he'd be on the back porch calling Maggie in.

"What are you doing here?" she asked. She lifted the lid of the garbage can and dropped the bag in.

146

"I've brought you a gift. It's from the museum."
He put something on the lid of the trash can.

"You got there after all? At night?"

Donnie didn't reply.

"What is it?" She gingerly took a small box into
her hand. Up close, Donnie looked worried, his face
made garish by shadows. His eyes were dark and
intense.

"An amulet. Wait till you get inside to open it,"
he said.

"But how did you get it?"

Donnie said nothing. Suddenly Maggie felt afraid.
She thought she knew Donnie, but now he seemed
different. Maybe he had met Morgan and come
under a powerful spell. She heard the back door
open. "Here comes my dad," she said. Donnie was
already going. He had turned away from her and
climbed over the remains of the chain-link fence that
ran behind the garage. The last thing Maggie saw of
him was his hand, resting briefly on the fence post.
A heavy gold ring glinted on his little finger—his
class ring, most likely.

Maggie ran back to the house, clutching the box
tightly in her hand. She ran up the back steps and
crashed into her father.

"Who were you talking to? Was someone out
there with you?"

147

"Somebody walking their dog."

"Who is walking a dog up our driveway at night?"

"Beats me," said Maggie, and suddenly couldn't catch her breath.

"What have you got in your hand there?" asked her father.

"Just something from the trash, looked like it got thrown out by accident."

Maggie dropped her hand to her side, as if what she was holding was nothing at all interesting, and forced herself to walk casually to the study. She closed the door behind her and sat down to look at the box. It was small, covered with glossy gray paper, and elegantly stamped MUSEUM OF FINE ARTS. She took off the cover. A tiny gold carving was nestled inside, beneath a layer of tissue paper. It was so small she had to hold it up to see what it was: an insect, maybe, or a tiny lobster. Maggie closed the box and shoved it down between the sofa cushions.

She reached over to turn on the television set. As the blur of colors slid into focus, she thought of something. In the fractured dark by the garage, Donnie's eyes had looked black; but she knew they were green. The very first time she'd seen him, she had noticed his mean green eyes.

16

MAGGIE WENT UP TO JULIE AT RECESS
the next day and said, "Hi," then couldn't think of
anything else to say. She had never been stupidly
tongue-tied with her friends. As she stood there,
aware that an empty grin still stretched across her
face, she suddenly recalled being in the burial chamber, holding the mummy case—she could feel the
smooth surface beneath her fingers as if it were happening at that very moment.

"Not again!" she cried. It felt as if the spell had
gripped her, and she struggled through the words to
fight it off. When she came to herself, Julie had
wandered away to sit with Penelope Miller and two
other girls on the stone wall beside the baseball dia-
mond.

Later that day, as Maggie was setting the table for
supper, her father came into the dining room,

opened the china cabinet, and took down the towel-wrapped bundle. He looked up from the stuffed elephant at Maggie's horrified face. "Well," he said, with a long sigh, "would you care to explain this? I assume you have the actual mummy hidden in your room? I hope you are taking good care of it."

Maggie opened her mouth to answer—this was another chance to tell him everything—but all that came into her head was a single phrase, repeated over and over: *the power of a servant, the power of a servant, the power of a servant.* She couldn't get any words out.

"Maggie, I can understand your curiosity, and your excitement at a discovery that could be so important. But I also credit you with enough common sense not to endanger what might be an important artifact of such extreme age." He never talked that way except when he was really angry. She tried to speak, but nothing came out.

"Maggie, go up to your room and get it. This minute!"

"I was trying to keep it safe," she said, but her voice squeaked and her teeth were chattering.

"The child is very upset," said her mother, carrying in a stack of plates. "Let's talk more about it later when she's calmed down. It doesn't help to frighten her!"

"I'm not frightening her!" retorted her father.

Maggie threw down her handful of silverware on the tabletop and ran upstairs. Once she was safe in her room, she sat down at her desk and tried to write a note to explain. Her hand was shaking so much that she couldn't read her own writing.

In a while her mother called up to her that supper was ready. When Maggie didn't answer, she called again that Maggie was to come down and they would discuss the whole problem later, but not while they were eating.

"Maggie's lost the mummy!" said Tom gleefully as she came to her place at the table.

"Shut up! I have not!"

"We're not discussing it now," said her mother.

After supper her father told her she would be grounded, and not allowed to use the telephone, until she told him what she had done with the mummy.

"This isn't like you, Maggie," said her mother, intervening in a coaxing voice. "In fact, you've been acting not like yourself for days now. Are you sure there isn't something you'd like to tell us?"

There is, Maggie thought desperately, but her ears were buzzing, and her mother's voice sounded far away and hollow, and she knew she couldn't break past the spell that was mixing up her brain and keeping her from talking.

151

Her mother looked at her closely. "Something really *is* wrong," she said in alarm.

Maggie nodded. Her parents both looked at her expectantly. But she shook her head and slid away from her place without eating dessert. She went back to her room and tried to do her homework, but she couldn't keep her mind on it. Finally she closed her notebook and went downstairs. As she was coming down the hall, she heard one of her brothers scream from the study—a scream much worse than the usual ones.

Spencer was sitting on the floor clutching his arm. Tom was standing on a chair, while the television set blared on.

"What happened?" Maggie's mother cried as she rushed in. "Let me see!"

"There—*there!* It bited. It bited with its tail!" Spencer pointed angrily. Maggie looked on the floor beside the couch and saw something scuttle into the space beneath the radiator. It looked like an enormous insect or crayfish—or scorpion. That was what it was: a scorpion. Suddenly Maggie was sure.

"Philip, look at this—he's been bitten by something!" Maggie's father came in to see what the commotion was. Spencer's arm already had a big red swelling with a tiny hole punctured in the top.

"A big bug!" Spencer wailed.

152

Minor put his nose to the bottom of the radiator and barked.

"Was it under the couch? What on earth was it? I wonder if we should have this looked at." Maggie's mother was frantic.

"It was a scorpion," said Maggie, but no one was listening.

"Will it come back?" Tom asked in a worried voice.

"He must be allergic," Mrs. Jones said. "He's having a very bad reaction. Oh, no—he's going!" Spencer got redder and redder, and his face puffed up. Then his eyes closed and he flopped over onto the floor.

"Quick! Get him to the car!" said Mr. Jones. "Everybody out of this room and keep the door closed." Maggie's mother scooped up Spencer and started down the hallway. Mr. Jones herded Tom and Maggie and the dog out of the study and shut the door behind him. "Maggie, you're in charge. Whatever it was, I don't think it can get under the door. Get the can of bug spray out and use it if you have to. But keep it out of Tom's reach. It's deadly poison. I'll call you from the hospital."

A minute later, Maggie's parents were on their way to the hospital with Spencer fastened into his car seat, unconscious. Maggie and Tom and Minor

153

were left behind in the kitchen. Maggie locked the back door. On second thought, she unlocked it. What if that thing was still in the house and came out to find them? They needed to be able to run.

Tom came over and stood next to her. "That bug that bit him, will it get me, too?" Worry made his eyes bright.

"Course not." Her voice sounded shivery.

"I don't want to go back in there." He put his hand in hers.

"You don't have to. I'll just make sure it's gone." She tiptoed down the hall and cautiously opened the study door. Minor pushed past her legs into the room. The television set was still blaring away. She darted in and turned it off. In the silence she heard the *ping* ing of the television cooling down, and then another, softer sound, like something gently scratching.

Her eye fell on the corner of the couch. She went over and reached down beside the end cushion and pulled out the gray box. It was torn to shreds, and the amulet was gone.

Minor stuck his nose in the remains of the box and shook his tail vigorously.

"Minor! Did you do this?"

Maggie dropped the box and ran from the room, calling Minor into the kitchen and slamming the

154

door behind her. "Let's stay in the kitchen," she said to Tom. "We can watch TV." She pulled two chairs up to the table and got the can of insect poison down from the top shelf of the cleaning closet. Then she put it far back on the kitchen counter, with the skull and crossbones facing out. "If we have to, we'll spray it with this," Maggie said. "But don't touch it. It's poison."

"It was this big," Tom said. He shaped his hands into a circle the size of a baseball. "It came right out of the cushion."

"Let's not talk about it. When Mom and Dad get home, they'll catch that old bug."

"But how will they?"

"Use some of the poison spray. Or stomp on it with their feet. Hit it with a broom. Or a shovel."

"That's it!" Tom gave a nervous laugh. "Smush it flat! Chop it in two!"

"Right!" Maggie gave him a hug. She looked down at Tom's bare toes. "Why don't we keep our feet up?" she said. She pushed two other chairs together and patted them for Minor. "Here, boy. Up here!" Minor hesitated, then hopped up on the chairs and settled down with his tail curled around his haunches. She and Tom sat on the kitchen table with their feet on chairs and watched television until Tom couldn't stay awake any longer. He put his head down and went to sleep in a pretzel-like heap. Maggie went to the linen closet and got two knitted afghans and spread them over him. She went to the kitchen phone and dialed Donnie's number. He was out, his aunt reported. "Could you tell him Maggie called?" she asked. "Tell him it's really important. I'll try again."

She sat back down in front of the television. She felt safer with voices talking.

Sometime later her father shook her gently to wake her up. "Is he okay?" she asked.

"We'll know more in the morning. Your mother is staying at the hospital. You didn't see it again, did you?"

"No, but, Dad, it was a scorpion. Tell them I saw a scorpion."

"A scorpion? They live where it's hot and dry, like Arizona. Are you sure?"

"Positive."

"I wish you'd said so earlier."

"I did, but you and Mom were rushing around getting him to the car."

"I'll give them a call now," her father said. "Maybe it will make a difference."

He picked up Tom and carried him off to his room. As Maggie started upstairs for bed, she heard her father dialing the telephone.

156

17

THAT WEEKEND MAGGIE'S PARENTS took turns watching over Spencer at the hospital. Each time the one on duty came home, Maggie waited to hear that Spencer had snapped out of it; but the only news was that he was delirious, or that his fever had spiked. Mr. Jones had called an exterminator, who came first thing Saturday morning. The man went through the entire house, including the empty doctors' apartment, but all he found was an old wasps' nest. "Whatever it was stung him, no sign of it now," he told Mr. Jones. "You can be sure it's not here. Any scorpion's nest and I'd have found it. I sprayed your basement anyhow."

Every now and then, Maggie went out and stood in the backyard and looked across to Mrs. Wilkins's house. Hadn't Thutmose said it took three days for a scorpion's sting to kill a child? But that was in ancient

157

times. The doctors would make Spencer get well, she told herself. She wished she could call up Julie, but they weren't friends now the way they had been.

On Monday morning Maggie's father said she had to go to school as usual. "I'll call Berenice Cooper and see if she can take Tom." The telephone rang. Maggie's father picked it up, and as he listened, Maggie saw his face lose all its expression. She knew it was her mother. "I'll be over," he said in a small voice. "I'll call Berenice right now. Yes. Good-bye."

"Spencer's in a coma," he said softly to Maggie and Tom.

"Does that hurt?" asked Tom.

"It's like being asleep, only no one can wake you up. Now go on into the bathroom, Tom, before someone else needs it."

Tom wandered down the hall.

"He's going to get well, though, isn't he?" asked Maggie when Tom had closed the door. "Not like Mrs. Wilkins."

"They don't know what bit Mrs. Wilkins. They've given Spencer medicine to make the poison go away, but it isn't working just yet."

"Don't they have some kind of all-around antipoison stuff?" asked Maggie.

"No such magic," said Mr. Jones.

*   *   *

158

Maggie used the school pay phone again at recess. Donnie's aunt said she hadn't seen him since early morning.

"What time will he be home? It's so important."

"I'm not sure. He didn't tell me where he was going after school."

"Would you just tell him Maggie called?" she said.

The wavery feeling in Maggie's stomach was getting worse. "Spencer's sick, he's in the hospital," she managed to say to Julie as they were going back into the school building.

"What's wrong with him?"

"They don't know. Something stung him. Some kind of poisonous bug."

"Maybe a black-widow spider bit him," said Penelope Miller. She had come up close behind them. "They can kill you, you know."

During silent reading Maggie thought she heard a rustling sound, or a scratching sound, like someone writing. She turned around to check the desk behind her, but Alex wasn't even holding a pencil, he was making spitballs.

She took a deep breath. Maybe when her dad came to pick her up, he'd say that Spencer was fine. That could happen.

Chilly dread made her tight as a drum. She couldn't keep her mind on anything.

She must have been making noises unawares, because now Mrs. Garber was beside her, resting her hand on Maggie's shoulder. "What's the trouble?" Mrs. Garber's eyes were interested, sympathetic.

Maggie shook her head.

"You've been sitting here sighing, and you look as if something is bothering you. Want to step out for a minute and tell me? Come on." Mrs. Garber didn't give her time to refuse. They stood in the hall. "My little brother got stung by something Friday night," Maggie choked out, "and now he's in the hospital."

"No wonder you're upset! Gosh—I wish I'd known that at the beginning of the day. Do you want to call home?"

Maggie shook her head. "There's nobody home. My mom and dad are at the hospital."

"Well, don't worry about your schoolwork for now. First things first. I'm sure the doctors will know what to do. Maggie? Are you okay?"

Mrs. Garber looked questioningly into Maggie's face, but Maggie's eyes were fixed beyond her teacher, on one of the narrow gray lockers that lined the hall. Just beneath it she saw a golden claw, a head with tiny beads for eyes, a segmented body. It hesitated by the locker, its feelers waving in all directions.

*　*　*

Mrs. Garber waited with Maggie outside the school building at dismissal time. When Mr. Jones drove up, Mrs. Garber stepped forward to open the car door for Maggie. "I don't think Maggie's feeling well, Mr. Jones," she said. "She's upset about her brother. She even thought she saw one of the insects—it was an insect that stung him?—in the corridor outside the classroom. How is he doing?"

Her father's face was grayish, Maggie saw as she slid into the front seat. He scarcely moved his lips to answer, "Not much news. Maybe tomorrow we'll know. He hasn't responded to any of the treatments."

Mrs. Garber shut the car door. "If there's anything I can do, please let me know."

Maggie nodded and pushed down the lock button on her door. Her father didn't say a word until they were home. "I'm going back to the hospital. First I'll pick up Tom from Berenice's. I'll bring him back here, and then I'll be home in time for supper—we'll get a pizza, I guess. Can you watch Tom for that long?"

"You won't be gone tonight, too, will you?"

"Probably Mom will come home, and I'll stay with Spencer tonight."

Maggie watched her father walk down the driveway. Minor stood beside her, whining. As soon as her father's suit was out of sight, Maggie wished she had gone with him. She went indoors and listened to the sounds of the empty house. The stove clock hummed, a board creaked, something ticked. There was a loud crash as ice slid into the defrosting tray in the refrigerator. And then she heard the scratching sound again, this time close by, in the walls somewhere. . . .

Maggie dashed up the back stairs to her room, slammed the door, threw herself onto her bed, and pulled a pillow over her head. All she could hear was rushing static in her ears and her heartbeat thumping in her head. Then there came a whispering *flap,* which she heard even through the pillow. A breath of air moved across her legs. After a moment she lifted the pillow an inch and peered around. She saw nothing in her room. But her closet door was open, and from it came a rustling sound. She slid off her bed and inched over to the closet. In the shadows of the topmost shelves she made out the *ba-* bird's shape.

"Thutmose?"

"Don't come any closer! You said you were my friend before, and look what happened. Why did you do that? I came to find out."

"I didn't want to—I was under a spell. But I shook it off. Now something awful has happened. A scor-

162

pion stung my brother, and he's in the hospital. What am I going to do? He may die!"

"What if he does?"

"Well—it's not his time yet!" Maggie sputtered. "Can't you remember anything that could cure him? You said there used to be lots of scorpions in Egypt."

"He should have had an ivory wand on his pillow, or an amulet. Too bad he didn't have a magic amulet."

"We did have an amulet—my friend brought me one. It was shaped like a scorpion, and now it's gone."

There was a silence. Then Thutmose said, "I remember one of my uncle's best tricks was to take a tiny carving, like an ivory crocodile, and give it to someone he knew was dangerous and pretend that it was a token of friendship. Then, later on, when the person had taken it home, the carving would come to life and get bigger and bigger."

Maggie's voice was squeezed to a whisper. "One of his best tricks? Did it have to be ivory?"

"It could be anything—gold, wood, clay. He used to brag that he was the only magician in the world that could do that trick. Others tried, but they always failed."

For a moment Maggie thought she saw the museum basement again, the scrolls and rows of closed boxes, thick with dust, and Seth Morgan standing too close to her, smelling of strange perfume.

"You know, Mrs. Wilkins thought it was your uncle who put the scorpion on your pillow," she said. "I think it was him, too, and not only that, he's still around here. Your uncle hasn't gone through to the Afterlife, either."

Feathers whirred, and the *ba*-bird shifted its feet anxiously on the closet pole. "He was teaching me to be a king."

"You have to go through, Thutmose, or you might not have another chance. You know you have to do it!"

Thutmose's wings stretched wide, and then he snapped them in close to his body. "I didn't want to believe it when Mrs. Wilkins told me. How could he have only been pretending to love me? And all that time I trusted him. I should have listened to my grandmother."

"You did listen to your grandmother. Probably you wouldn't still be here today if you didn't have your doubts, somehow. But now it's time for you to go through, to that Hall of Judgment. Tell the gods. And you have to go fast, because I'm going to do what he wants, if that's what will save my brother."

When Thutmose spoke again his voice was different, somber. "I must hear the truth from my uncle. I want to hear him say that he killed the true pharaoh."

"Don't wait any longer," Maggie begged. "Just go through, now, right now, this very day. You have the scrolls that tell you what to say. You won't make any mistakes."

"I saw the Underworld. I went a little way into it, just to see what it looked like. I saw you and the boy—I thought you were ghosts and you were already dead, and the three of us would be together. But now I know you're not."

"You have to go through the Underworld alone," said Maggie. "You *are* a true pharaoh. You will have the courage. Everyone has to go on alone sometime."

"Maggie, are you talking to yourself?" said her father. He put his head into the closet. Maggie whirled around, and Thutmose was gone. Tom was clinging to his father's hand, and Minor was just coming up the stairs. "I'm going back to the hospital. I'll call you in an hour or so," said Mr. Jones.

"Okay," said Maggie. She heard her father going down the steps, and then the car door slammed. Her room was empty now. She and Tom and Minor went downstairs, and Maggie relocked the back door. They were alone.

165

18

MAGGIE TURNED ON THE KITCHEN
television set. A spunky orphan was calling forth
canned laughter, and Maggie felt protected by the
noise. She switched on all the kitchen lights, too.

"Can I have something to eat?" asked Tom.

"What do you want?"

"I don't know."

"How about if I make some popcorn?"

"Okay."

Maggie hesitated before she opened the bottom
cabinet door where the popcorn-maker was stored.
"You know what? We better put on our boots, just
in case that thing is still around here," she said.

"Dad says it's not," said Tom.

"Well, let's be on the safe side."

Maggie got her rain boots and Tom's from the
back hall, and they put them on. Then she opened

the cabinet, got the popper, and slammed the door shut. Tom looked at her.

"Are you mad at me?" he asked.

"Nope. Just in a hurry."

Minor put his nose to the cabinet door and barked.

"What's the matter?" said Maggie, but she didn't want to look inside. She poured popcorn into the popper, got a large bowl down to catch the kernels, and plugged in the machine. It started with a roar of hot air that drowned out even the television. When the last kernel came flying out of the chute. Maggie unplugged the machine. She ate a few pieces as she set the bowl on the table.

"It's back!" shouted Tom. He grabbed her arm and pointed. "Look out!" He scrambled to hide behind Maggie.

An enormous scorpion advanced across the room, making a scratching sound as its claws tried to grasp the floor. Minor danced around it, barking, putting his nose up close, then leaping back as the segmented tail arched up and lashed at him. Maggie shoved Tom onto the kitchen table and climbed on a chair herself. *"I . . . I . . . have gotten power over the spells that are m-m-mine,"* she stammered, and rattled off the spell. *"The scorpion won't go any farther."*

The creature stopped by the table. Its claws waved in the air. It reached out and touched the wood of the table leg, then shrank back and folded itself up and was still. Maggie reached over to the counter by the sink and took a long-handled wooden spoon out of the utensil jar. She reached down with it and gave the scorpion a little nudge. It didn't move.

She jumped down from the chair and lifted Tom off the table. "What'd you tell it?" he asked, shrinking away from the table leg.

"A magic spell. Listen, Tom, it's time for us to get out of here. Wait, just a sec." She reached into the bottom of the cabinet beside the stove and pulled out their heaviest cooking pot, a big black iron stewing pot, and turned it upside down over the scorpion. "Now we've got him, dead or alive," she said. She reached for their jackets on the hooks behind the door. As she shook Tom's open, something fell out: a scorpion tumbled to the floor and struggled to right itself, its claws and thin side legs waving in the air, its tail snapping back and forth. Maggie dropped the jackets.

"Let's go out the front!" She grabbed Tom's wrist and raced down the hall shrieking "Minor!" but the dog stayed in the kitchen. Maggie could hear him growl. She held on to Tom while reaching into the brass bowl, where they kept the key to the front door. Another scorpion was behind the bowl, pushing it gently forward bit by bit as it struggled to emerge from behind. *"I have gotten power . . ."* Maggie began to shout. Her fingers were shaking, and she couldn't get the key in the lock. *"The scorpions will not sting!"*

The noise. Now she noticed the noise, coming from everywhere—a rustling and scratching, the delicate scraping of brittle shell on hardwood floor. She looked over her shoulder, down the hall, and saw a pair of scorpions coming toward them, scuttling along the woodwork, feeling their way. What if her spell didn't work so well? What if she ran out of power, or they had the power to resist her?

A scraping sound came from inside the coat closet. Now the scorpion behind the bowl waved a claw around its gleaming rim.

Maggie dropped the key. She bent to pick it up, and Tom wriggled away from her. Before Maggie could stop him, he used both hands to twist open the closet door, and she saw that the whole closet was swarming with scorpions. Dozens of them were crawling over one another: It was a nest; every coat and badminton racket and umbrella was moving, alive with claws and tails and hard bodies the color of honey.

The scorpions were swarming over the key, were scuttling across Maggie's toes—she could feel them through the rubber of her boots. She and Tom ran for the back door. They were both crying now. Minor was rolling and snapping beneath the kitchen table, scorpions clinging to his legs. Maggie tugged at the back door bolt. *"I have gotten power . . ."* she began again. Something landed on her arm. The little legs hugged her muscle and moved up toward her shoulder with a light tickling sensation. *"They will not move!"* she shouted. And for a moment, everything was still—a landscape of frozen scorpions. Even the rustling stopped.

Maggie picked the scorpion off her shoulder and flung it into the kitchen. "Minor!" she shouted again. But now he was nowhere in sight.

She couldn't wait. She yanked the door open and pulled Tom out with her. Behind her, she saw the whole mass start to seethe once more, as if given a simultaneous release.

Maggie and Tom ran toward the garage and the old cyclone fence. "Too many!" Tom was crying.

"We can get away. Just do what I tell you." Maggie helped him over the fence and through some bushes. "We have to run!"

"No!" Tom pounded heavily along beside her. "No!" Maggie half dragged him across Mrs. Wilkins's backyard and up the steps of the porch. She could probably hoist Tom up to the level of the window ledge and then sort of shove him through, if she could get the window open in the first place. Only Tom had other ideas. He scampered down the porch steps and across the driveway, pushed through a hedge, and sat down on the Harkness sisters' steps.

Maggie couldn't wait. "Just stay there!" she shouted. "Don't move!" She hitched herself up onto the window ledge, shoved the window up with one hand, and rolled through.

Maggie crossed the kitchen and raced through the passage that led to the front hall and main staircase. She knew what she had to do; if only she had done it sooner! She climbed up to the second floor. Halfway across Mrs. Wilkins's bedroom she heard a chuckle. Donnie stood at the door to the burial chamber, dressed in his varsity jacket, his hands jauntily resting on his hips, grinning. "Hi!" he said.

Something was wrong. Maggie didn't want to look at his eyes: They were what was wrong.

"Donnie?" she whispered.

"Sometimes," answered the boy. His grin glittered in his face. Maggie tried to step forward, but she was frozen; she couldn't move. Paralysis overtook her, as if she were encased in clear syrup or in amber, like one of those preserved insects. She tried her counterspell, but it did nothing. Her spells were puny compared with this one.

"Surprised, are you? Would you like to see an-

171

other of your friends?" said the black-eyed Donnie. Then Donnie was gone, and Seth Morgan was standing there instead.

"Or would you prefer to see me as I really am?"

Then Seth Morgan was gone, and in his place stood a dark-skinned man in Egyptian dress. His face was severe, and a gold snake ring shone on his finger. He was younger than Morgan, and his body was lean and athletic, not round and dumpy. His eyes were pitch-black. Maggie had seen them before.

"Magicians have the power of appearances," he said. "I am Set, uncle of the pharaoh Thutmose, and I can make myself seem to be anyone. Even you! Look over there." He pointed to the second-floor landing, and there was Maggie in her jeans, her hair sticking up the way it usually did. Only the eyes weren't hers—they belonged to the magician.

"That's the way I appeared to the O'Connell boy last night. He came here this afternoon to destroy Thutmose's mummy because he thought you told him to. Once he got here, I put a spell on him and ordered him to chop up the mummy. He's down in the basement getting a hatchet."

Running footsteps sounded through the house and up the stairs. Donnie came as far as the landing and stood there holding a hatchet in his hand.

"You can do the job together," said Set. He took

172

a deep breath. "And finally I'll be rid of him, *finally!* That will take care of Thutmose, King of Upper and Lower Egypt, son of the sun god Re, Horus the Hawk. He hesitated too long to take his Underworld journey. What a soft little thing he was! It used to drive me mad. He was never suited to be pharaoh, no matter how noble his birth. Son of the eldest son, a whining baby who became the ruler of all Egypt. He would get up in the morning and put on some piece of pleated linen and go stand in the courtyard and smell the sweet morning air, and know that it all was his. And he didn't even want it!" High over the magician's shoulder, on a carved beam near the ceiling, a small dark creature silently took its place, watching, listening. Maggie tried not to let her eyes travel toward the *ba*-bird. Set whirled around, and the *ba*-bird was gone.

"He's here, isn't he? He should come forward and greet his beloved uncle!" Set looked all around the room, but Thutmose didn't show himself. The magician crossed to the burial chamber and looked through the doorway. Beyond his shoulder Maggie saw a blurry place form on the other side of the coffin, and Thutmose's *ka* shaped itself into the boy with the royal collar. He looked scared to death, but he didn't take his eyes off his uncle.

"So we are face-to-face," said Set. "This is the first

time you have seen me, but I have watched you ever since I first found your spirit. I always took some other shape."

"I thought of you so many times," said Thutmose. His voice was quavering. "I would have given anything to have had you by my side. You were my teacher, my mother and father. I was afraid to go through the Underworld without you."

"I should have taught you more courage then. Unfortunately, it is too late for that lesson now." He turned toward Donnie. "You there, bring that hatchet and get to work. And you help him," he said to Maggie. "I don't need to leave a spell on you. All I have to do is mention your brother." Maggie felt the paralysis leave her.

"Can you stop the poison once it's started to work?" she asked. "Spencer never did anything to hurt you."

"True enough. Get on with the job. Chop up the mummy. I may decide to spare your brother, or I may not."

Donnie moved awkwardly past Maggie, as if the spell had taken away his coordination. She followed him into the burial chamber. He dropped the hatchet. "Got to lift this thing down first," he said. His speech was blurred and mechanical. He walked around the wooden coffin box to the head end and lifted it. Maggie moved to the foot end and pretended to try to pick it up. She groaned and panted as if it were heavy. As Donnie pulled it in one direction, she deliberately tugged it in the other. It slid along its stand and crashed sideways to the floor. The lid fell open, and the mummy case bumped partway out, its tranquil face smiling oddly at the wall.

Donnie picked up the hatchet.

"No! Don't let him, not while he's under a spell!" cried Maggie. "He can't do it right. He's too clumsy. Look at how he dropped the coffin. Give me the hatchet."

Before Set could tell her no, Maggie stepped around the mummy case and took the hatchet from Donnie's limp fingers. She considered hurling it out the window, but then Set could order Donnie to throw the mummy out, too. What was Thutmose waiting for? Was he still afraid to go? All she could do was try to stall for time. She raised the hatchet over one shoulder, holding it awkwardly near the sharp blade. "It's such a beautiful case," she said. "Why do we have to destroy it? What does it say on it? Does it mention you?"

"Yes, it does," said Set. "I wrote what's on there. It tells about a wise uncle tutoring a young orphan prince. An uncle who assumed the throne as soon as

Thutmose died. I did regret what I had done, but it was better for Egypt. I was a great pharaoh."

"So it was you who let the scorpion into my room?" asked Thutmose. His voice was steady now.

"I was responsible, and I commanded it to sting you until you were dead. But what of it? Why didn't you go through, you ninny?" Set's voice had risen to a shout. "Now it's too late! Now you've forced me to do this! It was a terrible day for me when I discovered your spirit was still at large. I had died myself, in my prime, though I did have many fruitful years, and I was just starting my own Underworld journey when spirits along the way whispered to me, *Where is your nephew? Your nephew the king?* as if you were still the pharaoh. I asked—hasn't he passed through? No answer came back, only the repeated question, *Where is your nephew, the king?*

"So I turned back to search. I was afraid if your spirit was loose, you might discover what had happened and not understand that it was necessary. Your grandmother had already made you suspicious of me, and I knew if you preceded me to the Hall of Judgment with a tale of being murdered, I would never get through myself, no matter how wonderful my accomplishments had been. I flew through eons of time on earth—I, too, have a *ba*-bird form—listening for my nephew's voice. You had been a talkative child, and sure enough I soon heard you chattering with that nosy old woman who was married to Wilkins. And she put the idea into your head again that I had done you ill."

"But you had!" protested Thutmose.

"So I killed Mrs. Wilkins with a poisonous scorpion. I still have a few at my command, as you know. Then that boy there stole the kitten mummy. I was able to convince this girl to bring it back. I lured her into the museum basement, and then into this house. See the pretty Egyptian toy?" His voice was mocking. He pointed to the floor, and a hippopotamus pull-toy appeared by his feet. Then it vanished. "I tricked her into doing almost everything I wanted, and you might have gone through at last, none the wiser—mightn't you, Thutmose the Utmost?—only the girl became your friend. That spoiled everything. But now she is going to put things right. Go on and chop up the mummy, case and all."

"She will never do it," said Thutmose calmly. "She is my true friend."

Set snorted. "Hurry up there!" he shouted at Maggie. "Or I'll strike that little brother of yours dead this very moment, and your other brother, too! You, boy, take that hatchet back and wreck the mummy!"

Donnie shuffled over to Maggie and closed his strong hands around the hatchet handle. She managed to hang on to it.

"You could have been pharaoh forever," Thutmose said. "I would have been happy just to live with my grandmother. But soon the gods will know you murdered me, and they will decide what you had in your heart."

"Nonsense!" shrieked Set. "Hurry up with that ax." Donnie was pulling on the handle, dragging the hatchet, with Maggie clinging to it, around the end of the mummy case.

"You won't go through now," Set said. "You're much too afraid. And you don't know what's really there. You think you saw the Underworld, but that, too, was an illusion I created. It is much worse than that. There's nothing there at all!"

"We'll see about that," said Thutmose, and he disappeared.

How long would it take him? Donnie was jerking and wrenching the ax handle. He'd have it in a few seconds. Thutmose would have to go so fast, reciting the right words, answering the questions at the gates. It probably couldn't be measured in everyday time: somewhere between eternity and a moment.

Then Maggie felt a jolt in the room. The floor

moved under her feet, like the briefest of earth-quakes. Set turned an ashy green and clutched at the left side of his chest. Maggie blinked as something began to appear in midair, a glowing, pulsing shape. It was a pair of shining trays suspended from a rod, and behind them stood a human figure with a jackal's head—the god Anubis, adjusting the balance of the trays. A heart rested in one tray, and in the other curled a single feather. Beyond Anubis stood a figure with an ibis's head—the god Thoth, ready to write down the results of the weighing. And behind Thoth a grotesque creature shifted clumsily on its haunches, saliva dripping from its jaws, quivering and snuffling with anticipation.

Set fell to the floor, his chest caved in on the left side, his hand clutched over a black hollow in his body. He began to metamorphose: He changed into a serpent, a crocodile, a beetle; innumerable Egyptian men, some old, some young, some dressed in jeweled collars, others carrying the simple tools of workmen, rose and fell away, one into the next. He became a black cat, the outsize yellow dog, an enormous scorpion. He became Donnie, he became Maggie, and then Seth Morgan; and finally the magician himself lay before them, his ring still encircling his little finger, his mouth opened in a soundless cry, and

19

MAGGIE AND DONNIE STOOD WITHOUT talking for some moments. Donnie shook his head and rubbed his face. "Are you okay now?" asked Maggie. He nodded. Maggie reached out and brushed her finger along the top of the wooden coffin, leaving a streak through the dust. They heard a banging noise not far off.

"So he finally did it," said Maggie.

The banging got louder, and they heard a door open. "Who's in here?" a man shouted. "Whoever's here, where are you?"

Maggie and Donnie went to the second-floor landing and stared over the banister at two police officers. "Here they are!" one of them called out. "Tell 'em we found 'em!"

The men ran up the stairs, shining flashlights ahead of them. Maggie realized it was nearly dark.

181

"Are you all right?" asked one. "Miss Harkness over there phoned us. Said she found the girl's little brother on her porch steps crying, and he told her he got chased by huge bugs. What's the story?"

"You shouldn't be in here. You there." The other officer pointed at Donnie. "We've seen you before, son, haven't we?"

"Say, what is this place?" said the first man, stepping to the door of the tomb and aiming his flashlight around the walls.

"It's a burial chamber for an Egyptian pharaoh," said Maggie. "We were just going to tell the museum about it."

"Just going to, huh? How'd you get in? What's this hatchet here?" asked the second policeman.

Donnie picked up the hatchet and turned it over in his hands. "We came in so I could check up on the place. I used to do yard work for Mrs. Wilkins. I knew she had something hidden up here, but she never told me what. I came by as a favor, seeing that she died and there was nobody in the house. Good thing we found all this stuff before something happened to it. Ought to go in a museum."

"Looks like a museum already to me," said the second police officer. "Now what about the big bugs?"

"They were at our house," Maggie answered.

182

"One of them stung my other little brother, and he's in the hospital."

"So. A big bug stung your brother, and then you came over here to look in this closet?" Both officers were looking displeased.

"You're not going to arrest us, are you?" said Maggie. "I'm supposed to be at home now, waiting for my dad to call from the hospital. And the dog! I had to leave our dog! I've got to get over there right now and see if he's okay."

"Sergeant McCafferty here'll walk you home," said the second policeman. "Along with your little brother. We'll want to speak with your parents. And yours." He looked meaningfully at Donnie.

Tom was standing on the Harknesses' porch with both the Harkness sisters and a third policeman. "There she is," he said. "Maggie!" He ran down the steps and jumped up on her.

"Everything'll be okay now, Tom. Let's go home and see about Minor. Those scorpions will be gone by now."

"You're the Jones girl, aren't you? Wilma Harkness." Miss Harkness nodded briskly. She gave Maggie a pressed-lips look and tugged at Tom's collar in a housekeeperish way. "I may speak with your parents later tonight. This is a brave little boy."

"I'm going to take him home now," said Maggie. "This policeman's coming with us."

Tom took Sergeant McCafferty's hand and they followed Maggie and Donnie along the darkened streets to the Joneses' house. Maggie ran up the porch steps and peered through the window into the lighted kitchen. The television was still on, playing to an empty room.

"There's none of them left that I can see," she said. She unlocked the door and shouted, "Minor? Minor?" They heard a whimpering sound, and Minor crept out from under a heap of jackets that had fallen off the coat hooks. He was licking frantically at his legs and sides, and there was a big swollen place on his nose.

"Are you okay?" Maggie rubbed his ears, and Tom clasped him around the stomach.

"What's he got—fleas?" asked Sergeant McCafferty, keeping his distance.

The phone began to ring. Maggie answered it.

"Maggie?" It was her father. "Where have you been? I've been trying to reach you. Are you all right?"

"I didn't hear the phone." That was true enough.

"Great news! Spencer came out of his coma just a while ago. He sat up and asked for something to eat. Everybody is cheering at the hospital. Turns out they were more worried than they let on. The specialist here, a Dr. Bertozzi, says it took his system so much longer than usual to respond to the medication that they weren't sure he was going to make it. And you were right about the scorpion! Dr. Bertozzi says it was probably Scorpionida something-or-other. He said it was very smart of you to have identified it. Anyhow, Spencer has to stay here overnight, but we can bring him home tomorrow. I'll be coming along in an hour."

"Wait a second—Dad? Are you still mad at me about the mummy? Can we talk about it when you get home?"

"Sure."

Maggie hung up.

"My brother's okay! He's well again!" she said to Sergeant McCafferty, who was leaning against the kitchen counter listening to her conversation.

"That's wonderful."

Tom had gone into his room and moved aside the cardboard blocks and now he brought out the bag of candy and perched on a kitchen stool and began digging into it. His face was still puffy from crying, and he took several shuddering sniffs in a row. Then he unwrapped a chocolate kiss, popped the candy into his mouth, and exhaled a slow sigh.

Maggie gave Tom a hug. "Dad's coming home

pretty soon, and Spencer's coming home tomorrow."

Tom looked into his bag. "I'll save some for him,"
he said.

"You see any more of those scorpions around?"
asked the sergeant.

"Nope," said Maggie.

"Then I'm going to go along. We'll want to talk
to you some more about the Wilkins house. Tell
your parents we'll be back tomorrow. You old
enough to baby-sit?"

"I do it all the time," said Maggie.

"So long, then."

The door closed behind him. Donnie gave a sigh
of relief.

"What did it feel like under the spell?" Maggie
asked. "Did you really think it was me that told you
to chop up the mummy?"

"I knew it wasn't you, because your eyes were the
wrong color. I went over there anyhow, and then he
must have zapped me. It was like everything was
happening underwater. I tried not to do what he told
me to."

"So that's why you were so slow. Thank goodness!"

"It was all I could do."

186

"If Thutmose hadn't gone through, we would've never gotten rid of Set," said Maggie.

"You never know—maybe he'll find a way to come back."

"Oh, come on." Maggie laughed, though for a minute she searched Donnie's face, as if his eyes might suddenly gleam black, and he wasn't Donnie at all and never had been.

"Are you going to get into trouble because they found us over there?" she asked.

"I'm not staying around to find out."

"Where are you going?"

"Florida."

"With your parents?"

"Guess so. There's no place else. When the police figure out it was me over there, I'd best be out of town."

She didn't ask why. "When we got into Mrs. Wilkins's house that day, were you really there to check on things?"

"Didn't you believe me?"

"I just wondered."

"If you want to know, I was going to see what was in that secret room. She would never let me look in the closet—she'd say, 'Young man, there are things that aren't your business!' So I decided to make it my

187

business as soon as I could. I went over to her place when I heard she was sick and went into the room there, and then I heard some noise, and I grabbed the mummy off the table and ran. Then when I got it home, something flew around it, looked like it had vermin."

"Must have been the *ba*-bird."

"Guess so. I didn't see it up close. I didn't want the thing around anymore, so I stuck it in that box my ma put out for the yard sale. Then I went back to see what else there was."

Maggie took a deep breath. "If you had had the chance, would you have stolen everything?"

Donnie didn't answer at first. "Let's put it this way," he said finally. "I'm glad I didn't."

"Hey, there's my dad!" said Maggie.

"Guess I'll go now." Donnie got up.

"Wait—"

"My aunt doesn't know where I am."

"When'll you be back?"

"We'll see." He grinned.

Maggie's father was just getting out of the car.

"Hello there," he said in a surprised voice as Donnie jogged down the back steps. Maggie watched him go all the way up the street, until she couldn't see his jacket any longer.

Tom rushed past Maggie. "Daddy, Daddy, scorpions were here! Everywhere! All around!" He threw his hands up in the air.

"I thought the exterminator couldn't find any."

"We had to run as fast as we could—run, run!—to get away from them!" Tom spluttered. Mr. Jones reached down and picked Tom up in his arms.

"There's nothing here now," said Maggie.

"You sure about that?" asked her father.

"Positive."

Mr. Jones shook his head. "We're getting that company back here, at their own expense, to check it out."

"Dad, I better tell you before the police come," Maggie went on as the three of them walked in the back door.

Her father stopped dead. "I guess you better," he said. He put Tom down. "Tell me what?" He took out his pipe and scraped ashes from the bowl into the trash can. Then he turned off the television and sat down.

Maggie put the string of events together as best she could: how Seth Morgan had given her the idea that the tomb might be nearby and that the kitten mummy belonged in it; how he had suggested that there was a surviving spirit from Egyptian times that would be lonesome for the kitten until she had taken it back. "I know, now it seems like such a story, how could I have believed it? But he just had a way of making me believe him!" Maggie thought her father was going to object, but all he did was light his pipe and go on listening. She told how she had looked in Mrs. Wilkins's window and thought she saw something Egyptian, and she hadn't been able to resist going back. She'd just happened to be lucky enough to have Donnie O'Connell's help, to get in the house without damaging anything, and the good news was, they found the tomb! The bad news was, they might be in trouble for how they found it. "But the whole lost tomb is there, Dad. It's been missing for years and years!"

"Mrs. Wilkins concealed it in her house?"

"It's all there. Will you call the museum? Will somebody tell them?"

"Of course. But someone will have inherited the house and the tomb, too, I should think. Here's what I'll do. I'll call the museum—it's too late now, but tomorrow, first thing—and talk to this Morgan fellow. . . ."

"No! Not him! He's not there anymore. It's someone named Fox."

"Whoever it is, I'll call them. You're right, they won't want a treasure to sit unguarded until Mrs. Wilkins's will is probated. Goodness—what a day. Now what do you want for supper? Shall we order a pizza?" Mr. Jones pulled out the phone book from under a stack of mail and old papers.

"Anything's fine. Listen, Dad. There's something else. When I took the mummy back from the china closet that night, I broke three of Mom's plates, the nice ones with the fruit painted on."

"I can't believe you did all that and we never woke up."

"Anyway, is Mom going to be mad?"

"She won't be as mad if you tell her as she will be if she finds out on her own."

"Maybe tomorrow after she gets here with Spencer."

Her father put down the phone book, crossed the room, and gave Maggie a long hug. "We've had a scary few days, and you have acted responsibly, and I'm proud of what you've done. Now, no more worrying for tonight."

Maggie nodded. "Get plain pizza, Dad. No mushrooms."

"Yeah," Tom piped up. "Get plain."

Maggie didn't want to wait to tell her mother, though. She wanted to be done with feeling uncertain. After they'd finished their pizza, her father called the hospital, and Maggie had a turn talking to her mother. Her mother was so relieved about Spencer's recovery that all she said was they'd figure it out later. "Spencer's turned into a holy terror ever since he woke up," she said.

Maggie and Tom were sent to bed early, and Tom didn't even argue about it. Maggie hadn't done her homework, but Mrs. Garber would just have to be disappointed. Tomorrow their family would all be back together again. Tomorrow Maggie would talk to Julie at school and see about patching up their friendship. Maybe Donnie would come by, though that seemed doubtful.

Maggie lay in the dark in her room, but she couldn't fall asleep. She pictured Thutmose walking all alone past pits of hungry souls and hearing howls of torment. He must have found his way. She thought of him giving all the right answers in the Hall of Judgment and telling of his own murder. And was he glad afterward? Did he find his parents and grandmother? He must have, but she wished she knew how it had gone.

Something else was unsettled for Maggie, too. She didn't know if she'd rather have it one way or the other, but she had to be sure.

She sat up. "*I rise out of the egg,*" she began, in a low voice. "*I have gotten power over the spells that are mine. My desk lamp will turn on by itself.*" Dark continued to surround her, though the moon shining

192

in her window cast a swath of light across the floor. Her spells had never worked very well on *things.* Try another.

"*I rise out of the egg. . . . The* ba-*bird will come back to my closet.*" She knew it was impossible, and that the *ba*-bird was not ever going to appear before her again, but she had to try.

After a few minutes she began a third spell: "*I rise out of the egg. . . . My dad will come up the stairs right now to my room.*" She waited. Her bedroom door was open a crack, and two floors below she could hear her father rinsing something in the kitchen sink. His footsteps moved back and forth, but they didn't come to the back stairs.

It was over, the power was gone. No matter what she said, she would not be able to cast another magic spell. She was left with only her ordinary room, the folder of newspaper articles she had once thought interesting, and her undone homework. Then she did hear running footsteps, but it wasn't her father. Minor came bounding up the stairs, hurtled himself through her doorway, and hopped up on the foot of her bed. "Good dog," she said to him, and rubbed his head. He curled up on the quilt over her feet, and they went to sleep.

20

IT TOOK SEVERAL MONTHS BEFORE Mrs. Wilkins's will was read and its instructions carried out. She had left her entire collection of Egyptian artifacts to the Museum of Fine Arts. The museum, in the person of Mr. Fox, was overjoyed, but announced it would take years to sort through everything. Behind the burial chamber they had discovered a hidden storage room with dozens of crates of ancient treasures.

In the meantime, the Egyptian department was going to set up a small exhibit and have a party to celebrate, and the Joneses were of course invited. By notifying the museum so promptly, they had saved the collection. John Fox had gone to the Wilkins house the day after Mr. Jones had called. As soon as the museum removed the burial chamber and all the other cartons, a leak was discovered in the attic roof—a disaster for everything that lay beneath it. Fortunately, by then that was only the bare floor.

Maggie asked Julie to come with them to the museum party. It had only taken them a couple of weeks to become friends again, and that was months ago, but every now and then Julie would still look suspiciously at Maggie, if Maggie started to daydream.

The person Maggie wanted most of all to come to the party was Donnie. He had never called her after that day, and when Maggie finally got up her nerve and called his aunt, she told Maggie that he'd gone to Florida. Maggie had saved the gum wrapper with the aunt's phone number on it, and she decided to call again a few weeks later and ask whether Donnie ever came to visit. It was the beginning of spring vacation, after all—she guessed they must have spring vacation in Florida, too. "I want to invite him to a party," she said. "And just say hello."

"Don't count on it!" said the aunt. "The last I heard, he's still staying on down South, though he doesn't get along with his parents. Never did. He's a good boy, you know—not like his older brother. He could always stay with me, I tell them."

Maggie and her family and Julie drove to the museum late on a Sunday afternoon in April. Julie was going to sleep over that night and stay for two more days, since they were out of school for a week. Maggie got butterflies in her stomach as they parked the car. She wasn't sure she wanted to see any of Thutmose's things arranged and labeled on exhibit, much less Thutmose's mummy case itself.

Down the corridors and through the galleries they went until they saw the sign with the pointing finger: TO THE MUMMIES. In the hall just outside the mummy room a big table had been set up. Pitchers of lemonade and plates of cookies were laid out on the table, and lots of people were standing around talking. John Fox, a friendly-looking man in a gray suit, stepped forward when he saw them. "Delighted to see you!" he said, and he shook hands with all of them, even Spencer.

Maggie and Julie stepped into the mummy room. Mrs. Wilkins's things were in a cabinet all to themselves, but before they were even close to it Julie had grabbed Maggie's arm. "There it is!" Maggie nodded. The kitten mummy, its wrappings restored, was in the front of the case with a caption beside it: *Mummy of a kitten, found in the mummy case of Thutmose. The toes are painted gold. Possibly the pharaoh's pet.* Possibly, thought Maggie.

It took Maggie a long time to walk over to the display cabinet that held Thutmose's mummy case.

"It's beautiful, isn't it," said her mother. Maggie made herself look at the eyes painted on the case, and her heart gave a double beat when she remembered the moment she had started to drag it to the window. But she saw that Thutmose's spirit was truly gone. The calm dark eyes were only part of the design.

The last thing she looked at was a group of tomb paintings, which, the caption explained, were put together from fragments of the original tomb walls. Professor Wilkins had stored the pieces in a big trunk.

Mr. Fox saw her looking at them and came over to tell her about them himself. "This one is highly unusual," he began. "It shows a priest or person of high rank, possibly a magician, falling into the open jaws of Ammit. And here—isn't this one lovely? That is the boy king Thutmose, sitting on the floor of a courtyard. Only it's not an ordinary courtyard, but seems to be supplied with every kind of food and good thing one would need for life. Perhaps it's a kind of heavenly courtyard, a courtyard of the After-life. What we like so much about this is how realistic it seems. The boy is sitting cross-legged, just as a youngster would sit today, and behind him are his parents and probably a grandmother, and see what he's playing with? A little black kitten."

"Are you feeling let down?" asked her mother as they drove home from the museum.

Maggie sighed and nodded.

"The Wilkins house is finally for sale," her mother went on. "There's a sign out in front. Why don't you girls walk over there and take a look while your dad starts the coals? We're having an early cookout."

"Want to?" Maggie asked Julie as they pulled up in the driveway.

"Okay."

They cut through the backyards and went up the driveway past the porch. The FOR SALE sign, with the name of the real estate company, was stuck in the middle of the front yard. The house looked shabby and abandoned. It needed a coat of paint and a family to live in it.

"Who's that?" Julie pointed.

Someone was standing on the front porch looking out at the street, someone wearing a varsity jacket with pale sleeves. Maggie ran over.

"Hey, what are you doing here?" she said with a big smile.

"What are *you* doing here?" Donnie said.

"You guys know each other?" asked Julie, looking confused.

"Let's say we had a mutual friend," said Donnie.

"Are you back from Florida?" asked Maggie.

"For now."

"You think you might stay?"

198

Donnie shrugged. "Haven't decided yet. But maybe."

"Want to come over? We're having a cookout. You can call your aunt from my house."

Donnie scratched his head, and his green eyes crinkled up in a friendly way. "Sure," he said. "I'd like that."